THE LAST FINAL GIRL

PRAISE FOR ZOMBIE BAKE-OFF

"Mixing doughnuts and the walking dead proves to be a deadly combination in Stephen Graham Jones' latest novel, *Zombie Bake-Off*, a slim volume of experimental fiction that wastes no time or word count on superfluous detail or arbitrary introspective riff-raff. Jones constructs a bare-bones horror tale by combining clever, offbeat humor with a familiar, yet unpredictable plot."

—RUE MORGUE

"Jones doesn't pull any punches when it comes to describing the zombies' relentless pursuit. He describes it with gusto and an obvious love for this bloody brand of literature."

—THE DENVER POST

"The narrative gets rolling with a good dose of smart humor and the uncomfortable weirdness that comes from inserting larger-than-life characters full of bulging muscles into the relaxed, Martha Stewart-esque world of ladies sharing baking recipies. Then it moves to pure, adrenaline-pumping horror before jumping to what reads like the best intellectual tribute to campy zombie films. The best way to explain Jones' prose to those not familiar with it is to ask them to imagine Chuck Palahniuk's blind bastard child with Harry Crews writing a funny, gory novel while trying to channel Joe Lansdale's subconscious."

—HORROR TALK

"Let the zombie mayhem ensue! [...] *Zombie Bake-Off* proves that Stephen Graham Jones has talent and style to burn."

—CHIZINE

"[. . .] if you're a fan of good books, well written books, and fun books that just so happen to have cavorting corpses in them, then you'll love *Zombie Bake-Off*."

—HORROR WORLD

"This is what *Twilight* would be like if it had balls, what *The Walking Dead* would be without the boring, whiny characters."

—MOURNING GOATS REVIEWS

A LAZY FASCIST ORIGINAL

Lazy Fascist Press
An Imprint of Eraserhead Press
205 NE Bryant Street
Portland, Oregon 97211

www.lazyfascistpress.com

ISBN: 978-1-62105-051-3

THE LAST FINAL GIRL

STEPHEN GRAHAM JONES

LAZY FASCIST PRESS
PORTLAND, OREGON

Dear Diary, my teen-angst bullshit now has a body count.

—HEATHERS

ACT 1

A wide grimy blade cuts into a neck hard before we can look away, the blood welling up black around the meat, the sound wicked and intimate.

Before we can even process the rest of the scene—it's night time, it's that cabin in the woods we all know, it's a blonde girl standing there shrieking—we back off this kill, come around behind this guy's body that's already twitching, is only held up now by the blade, we back off so we can see through the new wedge carved out of his neck. So we can see the blonde girl framed by it, her bikini top spattered with blood and gore, her chin moving with her mouth, her mouth trying for a word but—

Nothing.

The screen doesn't fade to black, it slams there, takes us with it, takes us straight to

→ a girl's voice, shaky like this is a second try: "I guess it probably started when that Halloween supply truck crashed off the road."

Beat, beat.

"I didn't even know there *were* Halloween trucks, right?"

Nervous laughter, the weepy kind, then close on this voicing-over girl's delicate white fingers twining her short blonde hair, and we stay there for the next bit:

"I guess that's where he got the idea, though. The mask, anyway. And then, well, we were just out there for some free costumes, you know? It was just supposed to be a fun weekend, and I mean, they're not biodegradable, would probably just kill fish—just kill the racoons—" but her voice is already breaking up again, because of all this

→ violence in the woods, that night.

We're still behind the action. It's exactly where we left it.

9

The jock who had his neck cut into, his head rolls too far over then folds back, is upside down, looking straight at us, his eyes still alive.

A boot chocks up on his thigh, pushes him down, away. Discarding him.

Then that blade—it's an actual *long*sword?—it points across at the girl, is Morpheus calling Neo in to spar, is Christopher Lambert being polite before the beheading, and we see what this girl's seeing: some complete freak in an unlicensed Michael Jackson mask.

The pale, grinning lips have had their redness scrubbed off but are locked into some latex grin, and the eyeholes are sagging, and there's more eyeliner clumped on, but it's him, right down to the red and gold letterman's jacket.

In case we don't get it, though, that Thriller baseline digs in.

It's chase music.

The girl's turned, is running hard through the trees, her labored breathing the main sound now.

This slasher watches her go, looks around at the carnage. The half-decapitated guy on the ground twitches and the slasher watches him die, is fascinated.

Once the guy's dead, the slasher steps past, after this girl, and we cut ahead, to

→ her crashing through the trees blind. Scratching her arms on the branches, crying, her bikini top trying to come off but she's just managing to hold onto it.

"*Help!*" she screams, "it's—it's Billie Jean!"

Behind her, the slasher hears this. It stops him. He looks down to his jacket, all around, such that we can read his mind: *Billie Jean?*

Still, this is what it is.

He slices an innocent sapling out of his way, steps through with authority, and, now, because of what she's calling him, there's some legitimate anger, too. Like, before it was just business for him.

Now it's personal.

Yards ahead of him, the girl bursts from the trees, almost goes falling off a sudden cliff.

A hundred feet below is a river, moving so fast we can even see the whitewater at night, and hear it all around.

"No no no no no," the girl's saying, casting around for a bridge, a hang-glider, a parachute, a zip line, a magic door, anything.

Instead, behind her something huffs air, announcing itself.

Something *big*.

She steps back, so close to the edge that the sole of her left shoe is in open air, little flakes of shale crumbling off into space behind her.

Is this it?

Then she sees the eyes, and they're too tall, too wide.

She's just shaking her head now, mumbling a prayer, making a deal, and it must be a good deal because what steps out isn't the next monster in this nightmare, but a tall, regal horse, its skin jumping in the moonlight, steam coming from its nostrils.

"Wildfire?" she says, at which point the screen sucks down to black again, taking us back to

→ her voice, coming from the blackness: "I hadn't ridden since the—since my dad, you know. I'm the one who found him in the stall that day. But—but he's the one who taught me to ride, right? But he's also the one who taught me to moonwalk. Or what he thought was a moonwalk."

She smiles, remembering.

We can hear it.

"Come here, boy," she says, holding her hand out. "It wasn't your fault, I know, he shouldn't have tried to ride you, he knew I was the only one who could—"

Wildfire stamps, blows. Isn't ready for any apologies yet, apparently.

But there's a reason: Billie Jean's standing there, just past the trees.

The girl backs perilously close to the edge again, even has to wave her arms, and's about to go over when—

The longsword thrusts out, cuts into her shoulder and out the back, holding her there, a drippy ribbon of blood draining down the blade to the cross guard, those drops plummeting down to the crashing river, the river pulling them instantly away.

Back to the cliff, though.

The girl's *trying* to scream now, doesn't have the breath anymore.

"I thought I was dead," she says in voiceover. "I thought that's why Wildfire was there. That I was in heaven. But Billie Jean had followed me there too, so I knew it was . . . it was the other place."

Billie Jean dials the blade over as if in response to being called that again, opening the girl's chest for more blood to pour out, the sharp edge pushing on the bikini strap now, like a blood-slick breast is exactly the thing we all want to see.

Still, Billie Jean seems interested, is acutely aware he's about to cut through that delicate string, is so concentrated on it in fact that he doesn't feel the horse's head, suddenly long and alien beside his own, those massive jaws practically resting on his shoulder.

He shoulder-butts the horse but the horse just blows.

Billie Jean hauls the girl around to the side, over ground instead of a hundred feet of nothing, and fixes his boot in her chest, slides her off his sword. Then he turns to face this interfering horse, maybe the only thing big enough to finally take him down once and for all.

The horse rears, slashing with its hooves, and Billie Jean has no choice but to fall back.

"*Kill him, Wildfire!*" the girl screams from her place on the ground, one hand trying to hold her shoulder together, her face tear-streaked, her bikini top even more tenuous now.

When Wildfire finally comes down, Billie Jean steps forward, swinging his sword like a baseball bat into shoulder meat, stopping short at the bone.

Shaken, he steps back, remembers his fencing.

He feints at Wildfire's shoulders but cuts across the face instead, a little slow-motion on that blade-through-eyeball number, the horse screaming in a way that hurts our heart.

"*Nooooo!*" the girl screams as well, reaching, having to *hold* her bikini top on now.

It's too late, though.

Billie Jean's going to work, is slicing into Wildfire from wherever he wants, just flaying the horse open, getting the other eye as well.

Finally he brings the sword all the way back to swing for the bleachers, go for the horse decap we're all secretly waiting for now that it's gone this far, but something's got his blade.

He turns.

It's the girl.

She has her bikini top wrapped around the sword.

"You won't write this part, will you?" the voiceover says. "I wouldn't ever take my top—I just really really wanted to live, I mean . . . "

The slasher, like he's scared of her breasts, takes a stumbling step back.

It leaves him just right at the edge of the cliff.

"And then I remembered my Sunday school," the voiceover says, and we're right there with her that night, her on her knees, topless but somehow not showing any skin, and what she's doing, it's some David and Goliath action: using her bikini top as a sling, a grapefruit of a rock going around and around.

"I guess I'm lucky I'm a C cup," the voiceover says just as the girl releases the rock.

It slams into Billie Jean's lower face, just *crushing* it

→ but the voiceover interrupts: "That's how it was supposed to go, I mean."

The do-over is in painfully slow-motion: that rock in her left cup, rolling out end over end over end.

For all her screaming, though, and even though she nails the follow-through, still, this rock, it hurtles past Billie Jean's face, and because he's a slasher, he doesn't even flinch.

His mask doesn't show it, but still, there's a smile in there.

At least until the bikini top reaches the end of its length, whips its string out like a dry tentacle, right into the eyehole of Billie Jean's mask.

Without meaning to, he flinches back, steps behind himself for a brace.

There's only open air.

"But sometimes you get lucky," the voiceover goes on, and Billie Jean reaches forward for balance, isn't going to find it.

He looks to the girl as if she's betraying him here.

"Moonwalk now, you fucker," she says to him, and he doesn't, can't. He just falls and falls, and, in case it looks too much like a sequel set-up, he catches a couple of shattering ledges on the way down, and, on the chance *that's* not enough, we go

→ under that dark water with him, bubbles and blood roiling everywhere.

It's that slowed-down moment when he's touching the stony bottom of the river with his back, hard.

An instant later, the sword comes down, right through him.

Above, on the cliff, there's a kind of musical sigh, dawn even starting to break.

The girl's just getting her bikini back on, favoring her injured shoulder.

"Let's go home," she says to her now-blind horse, and lets him smell her hand then rubs her hand along his neck to his mane, grabs a handful of that to haul herself up. "I'll be your eyes," she says, about to fall over herself, and we pull off this sentimental image, a girl and her horse, go higher and higher, finally

→ come down upriver, *on* the river, where that Halloween supply truck crashed.

It's still leaking masks.

"So he's really and finally dead," a male voice says, intruding, and we open up onto

→ a hospital room. The voiceover girl's there, shaken up by her own story, dabbing at her eyes instead of rubbing them. Because of her make-up.

A young, good-looking guy is putting his equipment away, just jabbing down one last note, an imposing Sheriff's deputy parked across the room, his pythons crossed over his chest, his haircut pure jarhead, and proud of it.

The girl's shoulder is wrapped. Her hair's been professionally done, it looks like.

"It was terrible," she says. "I never—I never—but it's over, right?"

"They only come back in the movies," the guy says. "If I need to confirm anything, I can just . . . " He does the phone-mime thing, obviously fishing for her number, and the Sheriff's deputy looks away, disgusted.

The girl nods, her eyes welling, her hands clenching the sheets, and, like we're ducking into her nightmare,

→ shuffling through the eventual police photos. All the crime-scene stuff. The camera-shutter sounds advance each gruesome slide. This is documentation of what the investigators found in and around that cabin: the girl's goodtime friends in watery sepiatone, six of them, each not just split down the middle or spiked onto a deer head or lying on the floor, their head turned around backwards, but some of them have been staged as well: piniomed in complicated rope-and-pulley systems that evidently dropped them down when somebody opened the door.

There's a head behind the medicine cabinet mirror, there's a cheerleader with a pom-pom in place *of* her head, each shot suggesting what it must have been like for our final girl, crashing through, finding all her friends dead, all her hope gone.

Finally getting to the partial decap job out front, we realize we've been seeing these in order, such that next is Lindsay and Wildfire, home at last, collapsed in front of a majestic barn—snap—then the ambulance carting her away, and then—snap—somebody in front of a grocery store, shielding their face with a magazine, and—snap—the double doors to the local high school, a wordless black banner draped across them, a sign closing school down until further notice, and—snap, snap, snap—finally a more recent photo of those front doors, stacked with roses and beer bottles, maybe a week's worth, and . . .

→ *snap.* The glare of the flash dies down and we cue in to what just got memorialized: a space at the top of a gigantic trophy wall in the entryway of a high school.

That space is sword-shaped. *Long*sword shaped.

Underneath, "Danforth Titans" is littered around, so we know where this 'sword' came from.

It's that reporter guy taking the picture, too. His nametag just says *Jamie*, and his police escort is towering right there, that same bodybuilder deputy from the hospital.

"So it's been a week and a half," Jamie says, looking *through* his camera, but, in

→ his POV, he's no longer focusing on the trophy case, but the mirror backdrop every other panel has.

There's students in that mirror, behind him, watching.

A studious girl in pigtails. *Snap.*

A tall, hot girl in a plaid skirt that's micro enough that it's practically a belt. *Snap, snap.*

A young Anthony Michael Hall, all the way in character— unfortunate haircut, pasty face, something about his posture confirming for us that, yes, he was born with his shirt tucked in.

Jamie keeps his camera moving, settles on the clear reflection of this one particular girl, streaks of purple in her cropped hair, Buddy Holly glasses, hoop in her nose, stud in her eyebrow, combat boots, probably something written in ballpoint on the back of her knuckles.

Snap. Keep her like that forever.

"So I know you can't tell me about anything active, Deputy Dante," Jamie says. "But can you confirm reports that the girl's father, in a persistent vegetative state for three months, went missing from Rivershead Hospital two weekends ago, and has yet to be, um, recovered?"

"Yeah, I'm that stupid," Dante says, turning around to all these high schoolers not getting to class. "Any of you delinquents repeat that, you'll answer to me, hear?"

The purple-haired girl jackboots her heels, salutes.

"We never heard you were stupid, *sir!*" she says.

Dante rolls his gunfighter toothpick from one corner of his lips to the other, and we get a hint of that lonesome Old West whistle in the score for a moment.

"You're new in Rivershead, aren't you?" he says just loud enough for Jamie.

"Just here for the story," Jamie says, clicking that shutter again. "A little quid pro quo, Deputy?"

"Trying to bribe me, son?"

"That's Latin, sir."

"You're going to fit right in," Dante tells him, shutting this operation down, and is the only one in the hall not to flinch when the bell rings. And keeps on ringing.

When the sound dies away, we're tracking along something . . . something strange.

It's jars on a shelf, fetuses inside, in alcohol.

Offscreen, some joker snorts twice, fast and pig-like.

This is Biology class.

That joker snorts again. He's tall, good enough looking, little rough around the edges maybe, kind of like Calvin all grown up, no Hobbes anymore to keep his bad ideas in check. He flashes his eyes up to his lab partner to be sure he's right there—it's that Anthony Michael Hall kid—then slashes into his pig fetus, a jet of fluid spurting up onto his lab partner's lab glasses.

"And that's why we wear safety equipment, people," the biology teacher says drolly, strolling among the tables, his hands behind his back.

The girl with the purple-streaked hairs sighs, takes her Buddy Hollies off, makes a production of settling the unflattering goggles on her face.

"I'm probably going to dissect into my finger now," she says to her lab partner.

"Brittney," the teacher says to that friend, tapping his own safety goggles, and Brittney pulls hers down as well, even though there's already cartoon eyes carved into the plastic lenses.

"Cute," the purple-streaked girl says.

"It's not about looks, Izzy," the teacher says, suddenly there between them, a hand on each of their shoulders.

"Is this about my nose ring again?" Izzy says, mock offended, but doesn't get to complete the gesture: some piece of a fetal pig splashes onto the table in front of her.

She tracks up from it up to that joker, wiping his hand on his lab partner's back and eeking his mouth out. "Jake," she says, kind of thrilled for this attention from him.

He shrugs about his lab partner, pretending it was *him* who threw the pig part across the room, and Izzy smiles, bites her lower lip in.

"Earth to Izzy," Brittney says, nudging her, reminding us once more of her name.

"Mr. *Stadler*," the teacher scolds, Jake shrinking enough that the teacher can catch his lab partner, doing something on his phone.

"Stuart Stuart Stuart," the teacher says, angling over to their station, his hand waiting for that phone.

"But, Mr. Victor," Stuart jerks, his elbow going deep into the opened-up pig, "I was just—I was seeing if you can catch anything from, from . . . "

This, his face. That spurt of formaldehyde or whatever it was, still leaking down his goggles.

"Might embalm you a little," Mr. Victor smiles, dropping the phone unceremoniously into his lab coat pocket then turning to the rest of the class, flashing both his hands by his face: "Ten minutes, people. Snip snip."

"So you been grief counseled yet?" Brittney asks Izzy.

"They're seriously doing that?"

"Just because it happens in the movies doesn't mean it doesn't really happen, know?"

"Like Lindsay and them even knew my name."

"So you're, like, not grieving then?" Brittney says, her cheerleader voice practically drilling dimples into her cheeks.

"Surprised they don't think I did it," Izzy says, making the first cut on their pig.

Blood squirts up onto her goggles.

She looks away disgusted that the teacher was right.

"What, do they pressure these up before class?" she says.

"I heard last year Jake put one in the microwave, popcorn setting, so that it wouldn't stop cooking until the microwave heard—"

"Ms. Daniels?" Mr. Victor calls across to Brittney. "You're not letting Ms. Stratford make all the incisions now, are you?"

"She's number one with a blade, sir."

"I love bacon, she means," Izzy adds.

The class chuckles.

"Five minutes," Mr. Victor says, spreading his fingers to show.

"This is going to leave a vacuum, you know?" Izzy says.

"This one little pig?"

"Savage weekend, Lindsay and them," Izzy says, cutting again, apparently at random, and not uncruelly. "They were the big fish in our diagram. But they ran into a shark, oops. Now our social order's all out of whack. There's going to be a couple of weeks before the good ship high school rights itself, not counting the week and a half we skipped. Especially in this pressure cooker called homecoming. When things finally settle down, the nerds will be jocks, the stoners will be cheerleaders, the goths will switch to menthols, the sluts . . . well, we'll still be sluts, don't worry."

"To mix about a thousand metaphors."

"I'm saying there's room to climb the corporate ladder," Izzy hisses, under the class bell.

"Since when are you the upwardly mobile kind?" Brittney asks, gathering her books.

"Since you wish," Izzy says, sneaking another look across the room, to Jake, dancing his pig through the air behind Stuart, about to nudge him in the ear with that cold wet nose.

"You know this is his second senior year," Brittney says, standing because class is over, her books clutched to her chest.

"Maybe he can help me with my homework," Izzy says, biting her lip. "I'm excessively stupid, you know?"

Brittney takes her by the sleeve, pulls her away as if saving her from herself.

Meanwhile, and even though this is the digital age, Izzy's photo from the trophy case reflection is in a developing pan, the rippling surface of that chemical bath becoming

→ the sun-bright surface of the river, an aluminum Sheriff's boat tugging through it, dragging a line.

Deputy Dante is steely-eyed and grim in the bow.

Behind him, the sheriff is kicked back with a beer, has a fishing line in the water, is reading a *Playboy*.

"How long we going to do this, Sheriff?" Dante says, extracting his latest toothpick from his mouth, studying its wet end. "Not like we don't know who it was."

"This is gravy detail, son," the sheriff says, turning the page and holding it away from himself, to see better.

"But—"

"Let the county mounties stay up there at the old Ramsey place and jack off into their test tubes, son. It's not going to bring any of those kids back."

"Neither's finding her dad. Sir."

"Shit," the sheriff says, looking over his magazine. "I come into town hauling that kind of trophy, I'm getting more action than the quarterback."

"Quarterback's dead, sir. He was the—"

Dante mimes a decap.

The sheriff shuffles the magazine down, leaves it way too close to the lip of the boat.

"Does Coach Johnson know about this?" he says, some real fear in his voice. "Who they going to run with now? Not that Tolliver kid, he's got an arm like a librarian, I saw him throw once at the end of that game over in—"

"Sir," Dante says, seeing the sheriff's rod tip bending.

The sheriff hauls it in.

At first—the music riding it for all it's worth—it's Billie Jean, but at second it's just that red and gold letterman's jacket.

"This might net us both some tail, Deputy."

Dante looks at all the water ahead.

"You can have mine, sir," he says, and brings the radio up to his mouth, keys it open to make their report.

Tight on two pairs of boots standing beside each other: the combat ones we know are Izzy's and, right beside them, tippy-toe, some distinctive cowboy boots, the kill-a-spider-in-the-corner kind, white with brown toes, brown heel cups. We climb from those boots up to Izzy's face in the wide mirror of the girl's restroom, Brittney right beside her, applying maroon lipstick.

"You're shitting me," Izzy's saying, adjusting her nose ring.

"What about the volleyball players?" Brittney says back, on a completely different track, it sounds like. "Where are they in this high school food chain?"

"She's seriously coming back *today*?" Izzy goes on. "Just, what? Nine, ten days after she was human shish-kabobbed? Don't you get an automatic A if a maniac killer stalks you for forty-eight hours of terror?"

"Just a flesh wound, apparently," Brittney says, popping her lips, "and of course she can beauty-pageant her way through the psychological trauma. Anyway, Lindsay Baker miss homecoming? Would the sky fall down too?"

"I never thought my high school would be *TJ Hooker*," Izzy says, disgusted.

"You think she looks like Heather Locklear?" Brittney says, parentheses around her eyes.

The answer comes from the stall: "Little miss obscure reference is talking about Adrian Zmed."

The stall door creaks open slowly and it's a drop-dead gorgeous woman of a girl, wearing a Catholic schoolgirl outfit that's about two sizes too small.

She's sitting on the toilet, angling a line of smoke to the levered-open window, an actual dagger in her hands. She's using it to idly carve into the stall wall, above the toilet paper dispenser. It doesn't interrupt her speech, though: "From *TJ Hooker*, you know? Think a slightly older Patrick Dempsey. Zmed got shot every other episode, but it never really mattered. Usually in the shoulder, too, just like our homecoming queen in-waiting."

"I'd say he's more like if Dempsey and C. Thomas Howell had a lovechild," Izzy says, not unimpressed here.

"I'd pay to see that," the girl says, spinning her blade on her palm, catching it cleanly.

"Crystal," Brittney says, announcing her for us. "Since when did they let you back in?"

"All depends on who you know," she says, standing, "and, you know. *How* you know them . . ."

Interpretative beat.

"Not Masters . . . " Izzy finally says.

"The *principal?*" Brittney adds, eyebrows up with disbelief.

"Good girls don't tell," Crystal says, sheathing her knife high enough up on her thigh that Izzy's

→ POV turns chastely away.

Which seems odd, but there's no time.

"And who's to say it was a guy in the first place?" Crystal's already saying, coming up to her full runway-model height so we can remember her from the trophy case reflection.

"*Mrs. Graves!*" Izzy and Brittney chime together, for the thrill of it.

When Crystal's close enough, Izzy takes her cigarette boldly, breathes it in as if trying to make up for having looked away from that flash of thigh.

"So you watch *TJ Hooker*?" she says to Crystal.

"Title suggested something completely different," Crystal says. "Isn't it fourth period, now? Second lunch or something? Is daycare not over yet?"

"Grief counseling," Brittney says. "Nobody's serious about attendance."

"Lindsay Lindsay Lindsay," Crystal says, sick of it all as well.

"Should have been me," Izzy says.

Both Crystal and Brittney look over, wait for this explanation.

"Just saying," Izzy says. "You've got to have the right backstory for this kind of thing, too. Me? I used to have a twin brother when I was like six. And when I was five and four and three and two and one, I guess. And fetal."

"You mean you didn't, like, *adopt* a twin?" Crystal says, obviously.

"What happened?" Brittney says, concerned, taking Crystal's cigarette from Izzy.

"Doesn't matter," Izzy says.

"Or you wouldn't have brought it up," Crystal adds, taking her cigarette back.

Izzy accepts this challenge. "Okay. This was before we lived here. Maybe that's the problem, you have to stay local for the rules to apply."

"You shouldn't think like that," Crystal says.

Izzy flashes her eyes to Crystal but rolls on anyway: "It was my dad's fault. He was drunk and stupid at the lake, dropped his jambox in, went after it, stayed down there hiding, being funny. But my brother didn't get it. You know kids, stupid. He went down after my dad. Didn't come back up."

"God," Brittney says, touching her fingertips to the hollow of her chest. "Why didn't you ever tell—"

"It's okay," Izzy says. "Good thing about twins is my mom had a spare, you know?"

Crystal takes her cigarette back, her eyes not moving from Izzy.

"So you're saying you should have got the slasher treatment, not Lindsay?"

"You miss your brother is what it is, right?" Brittney says, her eyes Oprahing out hopefully.

"Listen," Crystal says, running her cherry under the tap. "I know it seems like fun and all, and especially since it happened to a go-girl cheerleader bot like Lindsay Baker, but—" She twists the tap off, looks hopelessly up to the window she'd been exhaling from.

"But what?" Brittney prods.

"You *don't* want it," Crystal says. "Trust me, okay?"

"I was just—" Izzy says, but Crystal's already pushing past.

"I know what you were 'just' doing," Crystal says, walking backwards now, the suicide scars on her wrists obvious now. "And stop, okay?" and then she's through the door, gone.

Izzy shakes her head in disgust.

"Psycho cleanup, stall two," she says, and steps up onto the toilet, pulls the window shut, flinches when the bathroom door slams open.

"She's here, she's back!" that wholesome girl in pigtails squeals before moving on to the next door.

"The conquering hero returns to claim her spoils," Izzy says, stepping down, eyeballing the fresh-metal graffiti Crystal's left:

Inset, it's just "*slashers that aren't?*"

Over to Brittney, her whole posture about leaving.

"Like you're not going to go see?" she says.

"Everybody loves a parade," Izzy says, touching a metal shaving off *slasher*, and

→ they're there, at the far end of the hall, by the trophy case again.

"People, people!" Principal Masters is saying through his bull-horn, trying to maintain order but he's excited too, is considering himself Lindsay's very personal chaperone, it looks like.

And then there's Lindsay, in all her wounded glory. The meek survivor. The guilty winner.

"The final girl," Izzy says to Brittney.

Lindsay hoists her left arm up in victory and the hall explodes.

Masters has one arm around her, making sure she doesn't fall.

"Pa-lease," Brittney says.

"Shh, she's going to testify," Izzy says, and she's right. Lindsay is raising the bullhorn to her mouth.

"It's called witnessing," Brittney says.

"That's for church."

"Does it get more holy than this?"

Dead, dead quiet in the hall.

"I just, I just want to say," Lindsay says, "I just want to say that it could have been any of you. I didn't, I didn't even want to go out there like that, I was, it was for the raccoons. And the fish. I was afraid the costumes and masks would poison their habitat."

"'Habitat?'" Izzy echoes.

"Virginal *and* ecological," Brittney says.

"Got us beat," Izzy says.

"What?" Brittney says. "I care about the . . . oh. Yeah."

"Bet she just wants world peace, too," Izzy adds.

"But please, the focus isn't me," Lindsay says, and almost sways over. Masters is already there for her. "The flag, you all saw that the flags were at half-mast today. We lost six of our, six of our precious candles. But don't let their light go out. As long as we try to, try to exemplify their better values every day, then what they started can catch, can, it can become a *wild*fire, and change the world."

Everybody in the hall screams with joy.

"Can't say she can't maintain a single metaphor, anyway . . . " Brittney says.

"This single enough for you?" Izzy says, flipping Brittney off.

"You're so not final girl material," Brittney says.

"Maybe I'll be the killer instead," Izzy says, directing Brittney's attention up to Lindsay.

"No way . . . " Brittney says, but yes way: Lindsay's hauling up the Titan sword, holding it up like she has the power.

"It's still got its evidence tag," Izzy says, impressed.

"And please don't think this tragedy is going to, going to stop homecoming on Friday," Lindsay says, falling again a little. "If—if we let it, then evil, evil wins . . . "

"Is that President Reagan?" Brittney says. "Can you still quote Reagan?"

"He's the muppet one, right?" Izzy says, not really wanting an answer.

"Ti-*tans!* Ti-*tans!*" the people up front are already chanting.

Masters gets the bullhorn back, leads the chant like it was his own idea.

"Fuck me," Izzy says, looking around, impressed. "Spontaneous pep-rally to mourn the dead, or—yeah. To celebrate the queen, right?"

"*Titans!*" Brittney screams, just to get on Izzy's nerves.

Izzy shakes her head in wonder, in disgust, and then the chant dies faster than it should have.

The PA system.

Something's coming through.

Murmurs from the people. The sound of Masters breathing through his bullhorn.

"Stay calm," he says.

It's Billie Jean. The *song*. The drums then the bass, then the synth.

On cue, like he's stepping on a glowing sidewalk, a Billie Jean— red jacket, fedora, sparkly glove, Michael Jackson mask—steps around the corner behind Lindsay. At first we allow that it could be the *real* Billie Jean, but then this one's trying too hard, digging back for that signature leg kick, the crotch grab, the toe stand, then bringing it home with a moonwalk that traces a square.

Silence.

This Billie Jean looks up to the silent crowd, takes his poorly fitting fedora off and swirls it back on perfectly, first time, peers out through the eyeholes, waiting for the applause to roll in.

Nothing.

He takes the hat off again, frisbees it out into the crowd in disgust but holds on a fraction of a moment too long, so that the hat tags Lindsay. On her hurt shoulder.

She falls back into Masters' waiting arms, and Masters levels his eyes on Billie Jean about this, and a Ken-doll of a coach steps out.

Billie Jean nods about this eventuality and starts to step back, the coach committing to cut him off by crossing the stage.

Billie Jean turns around neatly, in rhythm, and weaves into the crowd, peeling out of the jacket, and, a few steps later, out of the mask as well.

It's Jake, from Biology.

He comes out of the press of people exactly where Izzy is, a burly woodshop teacher fighting through the bodies to catch him, the red jacket held high.

"Hey, girl," Jake says to Izzy, still kind of moving with the beat, which hasn't stopped. He makes his free hand into a loose fist, nudges her under the chin with his inside knuckle. "Purple?" he says, turning her head from side to side, to study her hair. "Thought it was white?"

"Different week," Izzy says.

"Guys," Brittney says, 'accidentally' stepping in behind Jake.

"Run," Izzy tells him, taking the mask he wasn't offering, and she's still holding it when the woodshop teacher pushes through, looks from the mask to her then back again.

"Thought you were taller," he says.

"I am," she says to him, and he takes her into the high school version of custody,

→ pulling her past the reception counter of the main office. He's about to open the principal's door to properly deliver her when the secretary is suddenly standing in his way.

"She's the perp," the woodshop teacher growls.

"Principal Masters is already occupied," the secretary says back, discreetly.

The woodshop teacher and Izzy look around the secretary.

There's a tie hanging on the principal's doorknob.

"Seriously?" Izzy says.

"He's attending to her," the secretary says, thinning her lips in insult.

"I'm sure he is," Izzy says.

"She'd probably be hunky-dory without your fool-headed antics," the woodshop teacher says. Then, to the secretary: "I've got to teach class, Marty."

"Birdhouses aren't going to build themselves," Izzy adds.

The woodshop teacher settles his humorless gaze on her.

"Mrs. Graves' office," the secretary suggests, rattling some keys into her hand. "She's doing counseling in the library for the foreseeable future."

"Lots of grief," Izzy says, and

→ like that, the guidance counselor's door is closed on her.
She turns the light on. Is alone.

"'I just want to, I just want to say,'" she repeats, in swooning-Lindsay falsetto, "'I just want to say that it could have been any of you . . . '"

She takes stock of this office again.

Specifically, the wall of lateral file cabinets.

"Except it wasn't any of us, was it?"

Cut to

→ Izzy shoulder-deep in these files.

Inset, we flash on her permanent record—it's thick, unforgiving, rubber-banded together—but now she's paging through the folder of "Lindsay Baker."

"Let's see what issues our final girl is hiding, now . . . "

As it turns out: none.

Lindsay's folder is as skinny as she is, just has pre-college junk in it.

Izzy rams it back home, chances on another: "Crystal Blake."

"Well well well," she says, and studies the door for a breath.

Nobody comes in, but there's something looming about it, the way it keeps being in the frame.

And, yep: keys rattle out there.

Izzy shoves Crystal's file into her shirt, sits back into a rolling chair and pushes the drawer shut with her foot, that same motion pushing her across to her assigned place in front of the desk.

It's close, and Mrs. Graves looks over to the file wall as if interrogating it. But then she comes back to Izzy.

"I was acting out earlier," Izzy says. "I can't, it's like I can't process it, all the violence. Maybe I didn't know how to cry, so I cried the only way I could, by trying to make everybody laugh?"

"Oh, dear, dear," Mrs. Graves says, and comes forward, is reaching to hug Izzy when Principal Masters is leaning on the doorknob, tying his tie.

"Constance," he warns, "remember?"

Mrs. Graves reels her arms back in.

"I initiated it," Izzy says, all vulnerability and puppy eyes. "I'm sure Lindsay needed a hug as well, didn't she? We all go a little huggy sometimes."

"Little lady," Masters starts.

"This is my office, Jim," Mrs. Graves says, and reaches a hand across to Izzy. Who takes it.

Masters doesn't like this whole scene, but all he can do is glare and judge, finally leave, making a show of keeping the door open, for propriety.

"Now," Mrs. Graves says, giving Izzy her full attention again.

"I keep asking myself, Why them?" Izzy says, something prim about the grin on her lips, and we don't really need to see the rest.

Across town, some sixth graders are fishing off a creek bridge. The bridge isn't covered, is just concrete poured across four wide, corrugated pipes, for the water to sluice through. Because we can't tell if it's the same river we know from the cliff, something comes floating past: a magazine.

The sheriff's waterlogged *Playboy*.

As it passes, the boys are taut on that glossy centerfold girl, her eyes smoldering up at them. And the rest of her.

"Look at the articles on that one," one of them says.

"Go go go!" another says to the rest when the magazine's past them, and as one they dive for the other side of the bridge with their poles, slinging their hooks into the water, covering all four holes, ready to snag this booty.

Except it doesn't come through. And it doesn't come through.

One of the boys leans down off the edge, just barely holding on

→ his POV searching that blackness.

"Who's going?" that POV kid says, hauling himself back up, his bangs wet.

Plenty of averted eyes, shuffling feet, bit lips.

"Ben?" he says, to one kid in particular.

"Pussies," Ben says all around, stripping out of his shirt.

He strides over to where they were, is getting his nerves together for this.

"We haven't done this since fourth grade," one of the boys squeaks out.

"Then it should be easy now," Ben says, and steps over the edge

→ comes back up in a splash, his foot already pushing against the concrete to keep from getting sucked through the pipe before he's ready, the water surging up over his shoulders.

Now it's scary.

But everybody's watching, too.

"Drop something to be sure," he says, and a handful of leaves flutter down.

Up-top, the boys race for the other side of the bridge.

The leaves ride the water out the other side.

"He's bigger than a leaf, though," one of the boys says.

"Shh," the boy he was talking to says back, then

→ leaning over, from Ben's unsteady POV, that leaf boy says down that "It's cool!"

"You don't have to!" that hesitant kid adds, cupping his hand around his mouth. "My dad, we can steal one of his if you want."

"Now you tell me," Ben mumbles, and nods to himself, pushes hard away from the concrete with his feet so he can situate himself on the surface properly: arms crossed over his chest grave style, so we're all holding our breath for him, don't want a *kid* to die.

But he does it anyway, pulls his feet together, the water sucking him into that darkness.

All we hear from inside is his scream.

On top of the bridge again, the boys are in a panic, don't know what to do.

They're all leaning over the backside of the bridge, where the water comes out.

"Shit shit shit," the hesitant kid says. "My mom's going to kill me."

"He's just fucking with us," leaf boy says, talking himself into it.

"Wait, look," a third says, and he's right.

Something's coming.

Slowly, as if grinning at them, a Michael Myers masks floats past. Then Jason, and Freddy, and Ghostface, and finally a whole dislodged clump of werewolves and zombies, devils and clowns.

The leaf boy jerks back, scareder than any of them, and what he finds for leverage, to push back against, it's the hesitant kid.

The hesitant kid goes tumbling into the water.

He comes up splashing, finds he's able to stand.
"*Do you see him?*" the leaf boy calls down.
The hesitant kid gathers himself, peers in

→ his POV just showing darkness, rushing water, but then

→ reversed so we're *in* that darkness, looking at him face-on such that he's framed by the mouth of the corrugated pipe. On cue and in scary-slow motion, Billie Jean erupts from the water behind him, his arms just like kid-Jason's, pulling the hesitant kid down.
Except—not down, but *back*.
It's not Billie Jean. It's Ben, fooling around.

On the bridge, the two kids left are rolling with laughter.
Until they realize a tall, dark shape is standing over them.
In their POV, it's . . . at first it wants to be Deputy Dante, but at second glance it's Jamie, the reporter.
"So all the water around here is connected, I take it?" he says, lowering a hand to help leaf boy up.
Leaf boy takes it. The other kid's still pushing back from Jamie, getting closer to the edge.
Jamie looks over, his POV taking in Ben in the river, removing the Billie Jean mask, looking up.
"What?" Ben says, a challenge.

"Do y'all even *know* any Michael Jackson songs?" he says.
"PYT," leaf boy says.
"More like Beat It," Ben says pointedly, clambering back up, mask in hand.
"That's evidence," Jamie says, about the mask.
"Of my bad-assness," Ben says.
"I can take it to them for you, I mean," Jamie says. "I'm going there right now for something else anyway."
Beat, beat.
"Or, I mean," Jamie goes on, taking out his pack of cigarettes. "I could tell him where to find it, either way. Tell that big deputy

I know some pretty young things down here have something they maybe shouldn't. I'm sure he won't mind knocking on a few doors."

"Dante?" leaf boy asks, his voice somehow cringing.

Jamie lights his cigarette, draws it deep. Shrugs one shoulder.

"How do we know you're not just going to sell it on eBay?" Ben asks.

"Hadn't thought of that," Jamie says, then switches gears: "You know, Lindsay Baker—I'm guessing y'all've imagined her a time or two, in high detail?"

Reluctant grins all around.

"She told me that, that right at the end—I can't put this in the paper, but she said she took her bikini top off, used it like a, like a *sling*shot. Picture that?"

He acts it out so they have no choice but to imagine her breasts, swinging.

"Bullshit," Ben says.

"She wouldn't," leaf boy says.

"She teaches my Sunday school," the other kid objects.

Jamie shrugs, not concerned whether they buy it or not.

He shakes his pack out to Ben, offering a smoke.

Ben, after a moment of deliberation, accepts the challenge, threads a cigarette up like this is what he always does.

"And?" Jamie adds.

Ben passes the dripping mask across.

"In the movie of this, nobody'll see your face in this part," leaf boy says. "You'll just take it. Be a shadow, like."

"See any cameras?" Jamie says, playacting a look around, then tosses the whole pack across to leaf boy. "And you found those in a parking lot. Same as I found this," the mask. "Cool?"

"Who are you?" Ben asks, in return.

"Wouldn't believe it if I told you," Jamie says, and, reaching for his car keys, manages to fumble his lighter out, onto the ground.

"'Oops,'" he says, smiling, and

→ a flame gouts up from a lighter, caresses the end of a cigarette.

Past it, we're looking down on the river, suddenly so far down there. And no longer in town.

Meaning this is that meaningful cliff Billie Jean fell from.

A signature white and brown cowboy boot swings into view and we sweep around,

→ are with Izzy and Brittney sharing a smoke, round about dusk thirty.

And, more importantly, reading a certain file, far away from prying eyes.

"I knew she was fucked up," Izzy says, taking a pull off the bottle they seem to have as well. "But this is beyond, right?"

Inset, in what has to be Izzy's POV, is a representative page of Crystal Blake's file, the rest of the pages kind of fanned out as well. Photocopies of newspaper clippings. Therapist reports. Medication list. No real details, but we get the gist.

Back to Brittney, trying to French inhale.

She pulls it off, holds her cough in.

"So are you Pink Lady material?" Izzy asks, not having to look up to see what Brittney just did.

"And who are you supposed to be, Fiona Apple?" Brittney asks back.

"Fiona *Apple?*"

"*Criminal*," Brittney explains.

Behind them, all around them, police tape is fluttering.

"This *is* like invasion of privacy," Brittney says the next time Izzy turns a page.

"More like *Invasion of the Bodysnatchers*," Izzy says.

"Which one?"

"The *Henry: Portrait of a Serial Killer* one," Izzy says. "The one where the freshman girl gets bodysnatched."

"*She was . . . an American girl*," Brittney sings, so perfectly on-key that it's spooky. "I thought serial killers were yesterday, though?"

"That's what they want us to think."

"So it's a marketing campaign."

"Shit," Izzy says, about the next page.

"What?" Brittney says, leaning in. "Spill it already."

"First, she's nineteen . . . twenty this week. *Tomorrow.*"

"Jake's nineteen."

"We're not talking about Jake."

"One of us isn't."

"Where she used to go school. This happened there too."

"What, somebody stole her permanent record?"

"Machete weekend. Bunch of kids lying to their parents, sneaking off to drink and screw and smoke it if they got it"—taking the cigarette from Brittney without looking up—"only they didn't listen to any of the warnings, walked right into legend. *A* legend, I mean."

"You mean Crystal's a final girl too?"

"I don't—I don't think so. The paper says she died early, one of the first ones. Flashed her funbags and got punished for it. A first-reel sacrifice."

"It says *that?*"

"I'm reading between the lines," Izzy says, turning the page. "And factoring in what we know of her now."

"So . . . she's dead now?" Brittney asks. "This is zombie high, what?"

"She didn't really die. Just got skewered for laughs, left for dead in some steaming pile of gore with her current boy toy."

"*That's* why she never wears halvsies!" Brittney says, so excited about it. "She probably doesn't even have a bellybutton anymore to put a ring in, does she?"

"Always showing leg to compensate for a little midriff shyness," Izzy agrees. "But it messed her up, don't you think? Wouldn't it, I mean, if you weren't ready? Maybe she really *was* a Catholic school girl back then."

"*Before the priest of blood found her . . .*" Brittney says in her best horror-host voice.

"And now she's here," Izzy says, closing the file gently, almost reverently, as if with a new respect for Crystal.

"And you are too," Brittney says.

"We all are," a male voice says, suddenly behind them.

Brittney startles around to a Billie Jean mask right at her level, which does about zero to unstartle her.

Without even thinking she shouldn't, she jerks away from it, *off the cliff, and*

→ would be dying already, definitely *should* be, except Izzy's stabbed a hand out, has her by the flimsy shirt, exposing one black-bra'd breast.

"What is it about this place and a PG-13 rating?" Jamie says, reaching down, helping Izzy pull Brittney in, his boot nudging their precious bottle over the edge.

"Lookout Point," Izzy says, straining to keep Brittney alive, and watches in instant regret as the bottle tumbles off into space, shatters. "Bare breasts are in the air. Can't get to second base up here, you're not even in the game."

"On three," Jamie says, and they haul Brittney in, deposit her as best they can.

"You're that reporter," Brittney says, straightening her shirt, seemingly as unconcerned about what just happened as Izzy.

"No, look," Izzy says, touching the Billie Jean mask. "He's next in line, the inheritor. This is the sequel."

"You here to slash us?" Brittney says. "We weren't even kissing or anything, I mean."

"Want me to come back in a few?" Jamie says, making to step out, give them their privacy.

"Show's over," Izzy says, standing with his help.

"Jamie," Jamie says, introducing himself, switching the mask to his other hand so he can pass them a business card. "I'm with the *Telegraph*, working the—well, this story."

He sweeps the mask around to encompass the police tape. That weekend.

"*Seriously?*" Izzy says, looking up at him in complete awe.

"Well, somebody's got to—" Jamie starts, but sees he's on the wrong track, here.

"What?" Brittney asks, peering over Izzy's shoulder.

Close on the business card: "Jamie Curtis, Telegraph," and the usual email addresses and phone numbers and faxes, all the area codes obscured enough we can't really guess at a state.

"Tell me your middle name's Lee," she says to him, tucking the card into her bra so that most of the card's still out in the open.

"And my brother's Michael, yeah," Jamie says, stepping around them to look down at the fall.

"Your parents were into horror?" Brittney says.

"She had other roles, you know?"

"They were, what? Die-hard *True Lies* fans?" Brittney asks.

"*Trading Places*," Izzy corrects.

"I'm just glad they weren't all into *Barbarella*," Jamie says, coming back to them.

"Or *Xena: Warrior Princess*," Izzy smiles.

"I could have been one of Charlie's angels, right?" Jamie says.

"Except they didn't actually kill," Izzy says, about the head Jamie's still holding.

He holds the mask up in one hand, lifts the camera from his chest with the other.

"Figured it'd be more dramatic out here," he says. "But, since I'm here, and you're—you're such quotable classmates . . ."

"Masters isn't letting you have access, is he?" Brittney says.

"We hardly knew her," Izzy says, leapfrogging ahead.

"But you grew up with her."

"Her, yeah," Izzy says, about Brittney. "I'm still new girl on the block, in high school years."

"So?" Jamie says to Brittney, and Brittney looks to Izzy for help.

"So nothing," Izzy says. "Listen, she wouldn't have—she wouldn't have got to *be* a final girl if she weren't pure, chaste, bookish, all that."

"She even had an issue to overcome," Brittney chimes in, telling us this is a conversation they've already been having. "'My horse killed my dad, I'll never ride again, but riding's what I love, especially since I never spread my legs for any of the boys at school.'"

"Not even for that—her boyfriend, the quarterback?" Jamie says, pen cocked.

"This matters for your article?" Izzy says, then shrugs. "Listen, if you're looking to bring her down, we're not the ones to be—"

"Just the opposite," Jamie says, writing.

Izzy glares at the top of his head.

Jamie feels the silence, looks up.

"Heroic terms are the only ones you can use for a victim who survives against the odds," he says, "especially one who survives what she almost didn't. What she shouldn't have."

"So you believe her little princess act?" Izzy says.

"It's not an act, is it?" Jamie says, flipping his notebook closed. "And it doesn't matter if I believe it or not. All that matters is what I write, and what my editor won't delete. Now, what about that other student you were talking about?"

Izzy moves Crystal's folder to her other hand, to protect it.

"None of your concern," she says.

Stare-off, stare-off.

What matters, though, is that Izzy, she's stood up for Lindsay, then for Crystal. Completely not in keeping with what we know about her.

She's more than just combat boots and purple hair, evidently.

"What were y'all doing out here, anyway?" Jamie says. "I mean, kind of a gruesome spot to kick back."

"Memorial service is going on right about now, isn't it?" Izzy says, and like that

→ we're there, swooping over the stadium. It's wreathed in tasteful lights, the stands are packed, and, at the center of it all is Lindsay, sobbing at the microphone. Everybody's hats are off, over their chests. Roses all over the field, the football players in their jerseys. Mascara smearing everywhere.

"Our kind don't do that," Izzy voices over, "we—

→ "—grieve in our own way, you could say," she finishes.

"Anyway," Brittney says, looking to Izzy for confirmation, "we're in the lull, right? In the saddle between the two peaks of violence."

"Between installments of this particular franchise," Izzy explains to Jamie. "Right now the killer's off—"

"You mean her dad didn't *die*?" Jamie asks, looking off the edge again, dislodging another slip of shale.

"Or whoever's going to, you know," Izzy says, about the mask Jamie's clutching, "pick up the mantle. They're out there planning right now, watching their calendar for some meaningful day, doing their cardio, making their hate list, getting their big speech together for the reveal, all that. Right now, we're golden, couldn't get hurt if we fell into a bathtub of dirty needles."

"Jigsaw . . . " Brittney says, fist-bumping Izzy.

Jamie considers this, considers this.

"You seem to know a lot about this particular genre we're in," he says.

"That's what I'm saying," Izzy says, amused by his ignorance. "This isn't a genre. This is, I don't know, if it were almost prom, we could have a little romantic comedy between slashers, you know? A break for laughs and love, maybe even a happy ending, with zero irony. As is, this is just an afterschool special. 'Don't drink, kids.'"

"Or litter," Brittney adds.

"Else you'll get accosted by the press," Izzy throws in, making hot eyes across at Jamie.

Jamie nods, digesting all this.

"And she *told* you it was her dad?" Izzy says, conspiratorial now.

"Read the article tomorrow," Jamie says, holding the mask up, trying to get it far enough away for his camera.

Izzy and Brittney catch each other's eyes about Jamie, Brittney dancing her eyebrows up like *Maybe?*, Izzy miming for Brittney to disarrange her shirt again.

"Here," Izzy says, taking the mask in frustration, holding it up over the big drop.

Snap, snap, snap.

Until her phone rings in her pocket.

She crabs it out, flips it open, has to flip it open three times to get it to work.

It's all cracked up, half-painted with fingernail polish, the screen flickering, barely holding onto any kind of signal.

"Seriously?" Izzy's saying into it. "I'm at the memorial."

She pirouettes to Jamie and Brittney on *memorial*.

Brittney starts fake crying, and Jamie fakes a coughing fit until it becomes real. He almost throws up, ends up with his hands on his knees.

Izzy hangs up smiling.

"What?" Brittney says.

"Got to watch the runt," Izzy says like it's nothing new. "You know, can't have any babysitter murders without some real live babysitting going on, right?"

"It's the lull, though," Jamie says.

"A girl can hope," Brittney says.

"Bad thing is," Izzy adds, looking across to where the lights of town are flickering on, "it's—she thinks I'm up at the school. Like, five minutes away."

"I can give you a ride," Jamie says.

Brittney hot-eyes across to Izzy again. Telling her *no*.

"Here," Izzy says, tossing Brittney the phone, then peeling her shirt off—Jamie shielding his eyes but definitely looking—so she's just standing there in her black bra and jeans, kicking out of her boots.

"No . . . " Brittney says, shaking her head but taking the clothes all the same, and then the file as well.

"Got a faster way?" Izzy says, then looks back to the biggest tree close to them, goes to it and, like she's getting her steps straight for bowling, she paces once, twice, to a certain point, and lines up along her arm with some landmark across the way.

"Got a smoke?" she says to Jamie.

He pats his shirt, remembers: no.

"It's just for the drama anyway," Izzy says, staring out over the cliff's edge. "Now you two lovebirds don't do anything I wouldn't," she says in goodbye, and corrects it down to a smiley "Anything I wouldn't *want* to do anyway," and then, her legs stiff and pointed like a gymnast, like she's really had that training, she runs to the edge of the cliff, absolutely *vaults* off into completely empty space.

Jamie falls back, terrified, his camera forgotten, but Brittney just shakes her head, tracks Izzy as much as she can without actually having to move.

"It's part of your initiation if you live around here," she says. "If you do it right, there's a deep part out there."

"If you do it *right*?" Jamie says, just as

→ Izzy *slams* down into the water, a human cannonball, and instead of tracking her descent like we did with Billie Jean, her splash is match-cut with

→ a long piece of red-hot metal in a dark basement with an evil furnace, somebody working it with a hammer, massaging it into the cruel shape of a longsword.

That hammer slams into the metal again, sparks splashing off once, twice, and on the third one

→ we're at the memorial service again. At the stadium with all the mourners, and swooping far enough overhead that we only know for sure that Lindsay's there. Meaning it could be just about anybody working that forge, making that sword.

And then all the lights go off at once, so the only glow is from those tasteful vine lights wrapped around the railings.

Out of the darkness, Lindsay steps forward with a candle, lights a football player's candle, and his flame goes to two people, then four, and in a few moments the whole crowd is holding a flickering handful of light.

Back to Lindsay, all that flame soft on her face.

She licks her lips, tightens her cheeks, her eyes glistening, and smiles as if seeing

→ Izzy finally surfacing, gasping for breath.

At first it seems she's in danger, fighting for life, but then she's just riding this out like a hundred times before, shaking her head from the exhilaration.

And it's nighttime, now.

The first one we've seen since the killings that started all this.

Izzy looks up into it, and we

→ come back down from it in front of Brittney's house.

Jamie is dropping her off, his car the kind of beat up that belongs in the parking lot of the Double Deuce.

"So did you, you know, initiate yourself like that, too?" he asks, leaning across her seat after she's stood.

She comes back to window level, giving him a clean shot down her shirt.

"I had to drink half a bottle to get the nerve," she says. "When you're an only kid, you feel all responsible, you know. For your parents' happiness."

"If you—if you hadn't made it, you mean?"

"More like their sadness, I guess."

"Your friend, though?"

"She's got a brother," Brittney says.

"Amazing," Jamie says, probably not about her jump, or Izzy's brother.

"Every few years, though, somebody . . . misses," Brittney shrugs.

"Why don't they just shut it down?"

"They put this iron fence up when I was in fifth grade, but the seniors that year painted handprints on it, for where to push off."

"And if they fill in that one place where it's deep enough . . . " Jamie says, grimacing just from the thought.

Brittney looks over to her porch light glowing on, a dour shape there behind the gauzy curtain.

"Speaking of parents," she says.

"And happiness," Jamie adds.

"I'll look for your article," Brittney says, and pushes the door shut, traipses across her lawn, almost skipping.

Pulling away, Jamie rights himself in the seat, and we see what he'd been leaning over, covering, getting Brittney to leave behind: Crystal's file.

Leaking from it is one of those newspaper photocopies: the only part readable is the byline.

J. Curtis.

An establishing, contemplative shot of the bridge those sixth-grade boys were at, and the angle on it—we know something's about to happen.

On cue, a shadow clambers up one side, looks both ways, then stands, crosses, steps off the other side.

It's Izzy.

She lowers herself to float with the current and we swirl downstream with her for about a hundred yards, until the lights of a nice house glow through the trees. The house is about thirty yards up from water, swirly metal sculptures rising all around it.

Izzy latches onto a branch she seems to know and swings easily onto the bank, then just watches the house.

"Mom, Dad, I'm home," she singsongs.

The yellow windows just stare back at her coldly.

She shakes her hair, checks to be sure her rings and toe rings and naval ring are all there, looks in her bra to be sure any metal in there's still in place—"God, I look like Tatum"—then takes two neat steps to a burly oak, reaches her hand into some secret crevice, comes out with another bottle, this one with pirate crossbones drawn on the glass with marker.

"Cheers," she says to the house, and drinks deep, screws the cap back on, wipes her mouth on her forearm, and what we can see from all this is how much she's stalling, here. How much she's having to steel herself to finally go home.

It's time, though.

She stuffs the bottle back in its hidey hole, looks back to a suspicious splash in the river

→ a turtle we see, somehow, like it matters

→ and then she steps forward, only the music is screeching up hard: a sparkly white hand has her by the bare ankle.

Izzy steps easily away, kicks free.

She looks to the house to see if this is a joke of some kind.

"Ben?" she says to the glove, surely connected to an arm that has to be connected to a body, but it's all so dark.

No response. No laughter.

And, so we can know who she's *not* talking to:

→ we're upstairs suddenly, over the shoulder of a twelve-year-old boy standing at the window, looking down at the river, a big distressed-wood letter *B* on the wall beside him.

Izzy maybe sees him almost seeing her, too. Or, she's coming back from having looked up to the house again, anyway.

"Not Ben," she says, as if checking off possibilities.

She straightens her arm to shove her hand into her wet pocket, comes up with her trusty zippo.

She shakes the water out of it, eases it open, blows on the wheel a few times, her eyes not leaving that white glove anymore.

She rolls the wheel back once, twice—sparks, sparks—and on the third time it catches.

Izzy lowers it and her face down, the fingertips of her other hand mushing into the soft earth.

The glove is connected to an arm, one in a blue sleeve that looks like it's from a uniform, like it belongs at a lube shop, a gas station.

Izzy follows it up, follows it up, to . . . Michael Jackson's pale, latex smile.

"*Billie Jean!*" Izzy gasps, falling back, splatting into the mud.

She fumbles the lighter away too, has to slap frantically around for it.

When she gets it going again—everything caked with mud, now—Billie Jean's still just staring up at her through his mask's eyeholes.

"Shit," Izzy says.

Billie Jean blinks once, slowly. As if saying please.

"Shit shit shit shit *shit!*" Izzy says, her eyes wet now—the girl who could never cry, she's about to.

She looks up to the house again.

"Can I keep him, Mom?" she says, and, of all the songs in the world that could cue up here, it's Michael Martin Murphy's "Wildfire," way in the background, already up to the happy lines: *She ran calling Wi-ildfire, she ran calling Wi-i-i-ildfi-ire . . .*

We're looking at a utility-room door when it opens.

It's Izzy, in tight jeans and black bra, dripping wet, purple-streaked hair plastered to the side of her face.

Behind her, the rumble of the garage door coming down, the whole house shaking.

Izzy

→ strides into the kitchen, her eyes flat.

She beelines the refrigerator, crams a stray glass under the cold water spigot, then, from the other room: " . . . no, no, I could tell what it was right when I first saw it, of course, I'm just saying . . . "

It's a male voice, evidently out of place in Izzy's house—we can tell by how Izzy cocks her head over to be sure she's hearing who she's hearing.

"You mean people line up to *buy* it?" the voice goes on, trailing off into a swallowed chuckle, and that's our cue to go

→ tight on a beer cap, twisting off in a pair of burly hands.

Coming up from that, over a breakfast table, it's the sheriff's hands.

He raises the beer to catch the froth but gets stopped halfway:

In his POV, it's Izzy, framed in the doorway. Dressed like she's dressed. Or, mostly undressed. Hair still trailing water.

The sheriff's beer froths over onto his hand.

"Here, here," Izzy's mom says, reaching across with her napkin, looking up to Izzy. "The sheriff was just appreciating my new hobby," which

→ delivers us to a lingering look at one of her metal sculptures in the front yard, lit by muted footlights. It's twisted rebar, reclaimed farming implements, burnished welds everywhere like a snowball from a junkyard, but, still, there's something there. Lines of intention, loyalty to some vision, a snapshot of Izzy's mom's mental state— *some*thing.

"Thought I needed to be here to babysit the runt," Izzy says.

"Sheriff Mills is just—"

"Going door to door to everybody whose property backs up to the creek," he says with all the booming authority of his office, then he finally drinks the top off his beer, not looking away from Izzy's bare stomach even for an instant.

"*Why?*" Izzy says, then looks away fast and guilty: she thinks she's given Billie Jean away. That they know already.

"Supposedly some kids found some of that junk from the Halloween truck," Sheriff Mills says.

"I didn't see your car out front," Izzy says.

"Just ambling, little lady. Taking in the night air."

"And you need it?" Izzy asks. "The costumes or whatever? It evidence?"

"They just don't want it showing up online," Izzy's mom says, taking stock of Izzy's non-outfit, now. "Somebody could dress up, get . . . hurt. You know how people are."

"Pitchforks, torches," Izzy fills in, so sick of this medieval village she lives in.

"Wouldn't reflect well on Rivershead either," Izzy's dad says now, from the opposite doorway. "Mobs, lynchings. Necklaces made from fingers."

Like Izzy's mom, he's fit but going soft, looks like he works in the corner office, looks out the window a lot, drives a car that costs as much as his first house. Or maybe doesn't work at all.

His arm's cocked high in the doorway, and casual in that hand is a mixed drink without much mix in it. It's full enough to suggest he just stepped into the other room for it.

"Must have been some memorial service," he says, tipping his drink at Izzy's black bra, then, to Izzy's mom: "Didn't Bobbie Brown wear one like that in . . . what was it? Cherry Pie? Remember that one? Real classy."

"Dear," Izzy's mom says, blinking patiently to show us Izzy's dad's drunk, and that this is nothing new.

"No, no," he says, stepping in anyway. "It was that, that Bobbie Brown in, in—yeah. That one Great White video."

Sheriff Mills is looking at him like the alien he is.

"Or was it Billie Idol, Rock the Cradle of Love?" Izzy's dad goes on. "That the look you're going for this month, Iz?"

"June, are you going to let Ward talk to me like this in front of company?" Izzy says to her mom.

"Father knows best," Izzy's dad says, sloshing down into a chair, peeling out of his own shirt. "Maybe it's the new style, right? What do you think, Sheriff? Sure as hell makes getting dressed a lot easier."

Sheriff Mills takes another drink, doesn't answer.

"She was smoking cigarettes down at the creek." It's a boy's voice—'Ben,' the sixth grader from the bridge.

"Ah, the one who needs *baby*sitting . . . " Izzy says to him, cutting her eyes at him hard, slicing her hand across her own neck to shush him.

"Is that illegal?" Ben says to the sheriff, staring at Izzy the whole time. "Can she go to jail now for underage smoking? Need to borrow my harmonica, Iz?"

Sheriff Mills stands to make his escape, lifting the beer bottle to show he's taking it with him, and's grateful.

"Just let me know if anything washes up," he says. "Got a lot more houses to get to before—well."

He tipsies towards the front door, leading with his gut.

"Magazines count?" Ben asks.

Sheriff Mills looks back to him, his eyes uncertain for a moment. And a little bit nervous.

"*Halloween* litter," he says. "Not the usual kind." Then, to Izzy, "And you should listen to your parents, little miss. About wardrobe issues, I mean."

"They haven't led me wrong yet," Izzy tells him, and falls back from her station in the doorway, to

→ the sink, to deposit her water glass.

"My life is so generic," she says to herself.

"You know better than to provoke him," her mom says, there behind her already, her hand trying to cup Izzy's side.

"Weren't you going out?" Izzy says, shaking her mom off, then running her glass full of water she doesn't want.

The *front* of Izzy's house is stately. White stone, good windows, manicured lawn. A pricey sedan pulling away—Izzy's parents—its headlights coming on as it gets onto the street.

Except, is that "Billie Jean" starting up in the background?

"Not that one," Izzy voices over, and we go

→ inside, to the living room.

She's on the couch in shorts and a t-shirt—standard babysitter outfit—and Ben's got the remote.

He clicks it again, away from the "Billie Jean" video, and, instead of going to whatever he's advancing to for Izzy, we take a lazy pan over to

→ the video cabinet.

It's a mix of VHS and DVD, heavy on the VHS.

We linger. It's all the Golden Age slashers, and beyond, and before, and besides. A horror library, so complete it hurts.

"Those are all for you, you know," Izzy says to Ben, cueing us in that it's her POV we're dropping out of.

Ben looks around to her, tracks to the cabinet she's studying.

"What do you mean?"

45

"Next year it'll be like a ceremony. You'll watch them all with him over the summer. Mom won't like it, but you know Dad. It'll probably work with you, though."

"What do you mean?"

"You pee standing up," Izzy shrugs.

"This it?" Ben says, stabbing the remote at the screen to stop it.

Inset on their television, it's "Thriller."

"He's a werewolf at first," Izzy says, "but then he's a zombie, but then at the end he's kind of got werewolf eyes again."

"And now he's dead."

Izzy shrugs like that's not the point.

"And we have to listen to this?" Ben whines.

"Drink your cough syrup."

"Nobody dresses like that in real life."

"Somebody is."

"Billie Jean?"

"Y'all know about him in baby school?"

"He's dead too."

"Well. Until the sequel, yeah. The really good killers always get a return visa to the land of the living. You'll learn."

"Life isn't a movie, Iz."

"Don't call me that."

"Iz, Iz, Iz. Wizard of Iz."

"He means 'Isadore' when he says it, not 'Isabelle.' And that I'm not him. That it should have been me."

Ben swallows whatever he had ready, his eyes flicking—for us—to

→ a family photo above the video shelf. It's from before his time, is Izzy and her mom and dad all happy on a boat, and, smiling right there with him is Izzy's twin, Isadore, the two of them indistinguishable at that age. And so happy.

Izzy again, watching "Thriller."

"You're the second chance, now," she's saying to Ben, disgusted. "He's already given up on me."

Ben's just staring at the screen as well.

Each of their reflections are there, ghosts stenciled onto the music video.

"Billie Jean," Ben says, finally. "It's from the song. 'The kid is not my son' or whatever. Some dad back in the dinosaur days thought his daughter's date had knocked her up, so he took the kid, the date, I think his name was James—"

"And your friend's big brother's teacher remembers him from chemistry class."

"—he takes him up to that make-out place and ties a rock to his . . . you know, mister dangly, and drops it off, and James or whoever, instead of letting the string . . . he jumps off after it—"

"Is never seen again," Izzy fills in. "Yeah, close enough. Except when that girl has the baby, it didn't look like her date at all. And the dad drops it off the cliff as well."

"Then it grows up to become Billie Jean!" Ben says, pumping a lackluster fist then letting that fist become masturbatory, his comment on this bullshit story.

"Recognize a theme?"

"The cliff?"

"Fathers of the year," Izzy says, obviously.

"If you're wanting me knocked out," Ben says, sitting up. "It's going to take more than this."

He's holding up the cough syrup Izzy's dosing him with.

"I could just deck you," Izzy offers.

"Where you wanting to go, anyway?"

"Telling you would defeat medicating you to sleep so you can't tell on me, wouldn't it?"

Ben appreciates that, but's wheeling and dealing here, too.

"Just saying," he says, and holds up his nearly-gone cough syrup, fakes a cough out.

Izzy stands from the couch, crosses to the obviously-locked liquor cabinet. No: liquor *shrine*.

"Tell on me for this, you're telling on yourself," she says, and pops a book neatly from a shelf—*Brains Anatomy*—and flips to a page, pinches up the liquor cabinet key.

"*That's* where he put it," Ben says, kind of impressed.

"It's always here or that urban legends one," Izzy leads off, opening the door grandly, "or just in the lock, depending on how late he goes."

She picks a bottle at random, dollops a shot or two into the high-dollar tumbler.

"Don't be stingy now," Ben calls across. "I might wake up, get scared, call Mom."

Izzy shakes her head, impressed, and sloshes the tumbler full.

Meanwhile, Brittney's sleeping in her bed—lots of emphasis on her absolutely *huge* (and unaccountably frilly) bedroom window— when her phone burrs in her hand, the glow kind of adding to the tension.

It's not a call, of course, but a text.

She pulls it to her face, reads for a few seconds then drops her hand.

"You bitch," she says, and looks to her window, as if sensing something there. Somebody.

It's just a window, though.

For now.

Back to Izzy's dark street.

Sheriff Mills is walking back, making his return trip from the cul-de-sac.

Now he has two empty bottles in his left hand, a mostly-gone one in his right, and they're all different colors.

He's humming, is pleased with himself.

As he passes Izzy's house he lifts his current bottle in drunken salute then kills it.

About even with their bricked-up mailbox, he looks behind him. And ahead of him.

Not for any threat, but to make sure the coast is clear.

When it is, he steps off the road a bit, into the ring of light of one of those swirly metal sculptures, and unzips, arcs a sputtering, pale stream into the twists and turns of the sculpture.

"You want modern art, I'll give you modern art," he mumbles, splashing it over as much of the metal as he can.

The way this is framed, too, there's this big empty space over his shoulder, so that we're holding our breaths (but grinning, be- cause he's so going to deserve it), and jump hard when, instead of some shape stepping into the sheriff's space, the garage door of

Izzy's house starts to grind up.

Its yellow light spills down the drive, almost to him, so he has to hotfoot away, trying to zip up but then an old-fashioned landline suddenly rings in Izzy's opening garage, so much louder than should be possible, and this is one startle too much for Sheriff Mills.

His heel catches a brick flowerbed border and he falls back, his hands still occupied (beer, peeing), and this incline is sharp, dangerous. He spills down it and down it, disappears into the darkness.

Inside the garage, under that light she evidently clicked on, Izzy's standing there, a twisty-corded phone stretched from the wall to her ear, some camo hunting duffel bag hooked over her shoulder. Still in shorts and t-shirt, barefoot, hair washed and pulled back.

"*Do you know where the children are?*" an altered voice says through the phone.

"You should come over, Britt," Izzy says, peering out into the darkness like she thought she heard something out there.

"*Do you want to play a game?*" the voice asks.

Izzy switches ears, hitches the duffel up higher.

"Listen, I'm the only one in this town who would get this like you want, and you're the only one who would know to call me at home instead of my cell. Doesn't take Colombo. This is more Matlock grade."

"*You've got seven days to live.*"

"Yeah, homecoming, right? More like two days, sorry. Big pig-blood finale, a little *Prom Night* disco action. Hey, you want to know what else? You'll like this. I know what you did last summer. And who with."

Silence, silence.

Izzy smiles. "Seriously though, I've got a surprise. This is no-joke big-time. It changes everything."

"*I like your red shorts.*"

Izzy looks down, *does* have red shorts on.

"Forget it," she says. "Don't tell me not to hang up on you either. It's already too—"

And she dial-tones the call, snakes her tongue out to it, very Freddy.

Now it's just her and the darkness past the driveway. She nods to it like telling it to wait and we go with her to some supply-closet part of the garage. The outdoorsy closet—how rich people do it, anyway. There's kayaks and skis and backpacks and water bottles and, on another wall, all the turkey-hunting gear one person could ever order from a catalog.

Izzy shops the shelves until she finds a mondo first-aid kit.

She puts it in the bag, steps out the garage door and uses the keypad on the wall to close it behind her, leaving her in some deep darkness.

She flips the keypad back up, opens the door again, rummages in the cute little coupe in the garage until she finds a stun gun in the console. She taps the trigger once, sending a blue arc of pain from contact point to contact point.

Now she's hiking down through the scrub, to the water glittering down there.

"Lindsay Baker my ass," she's saying to herself. "Any virgin can *kill* one. Try bringing one back, though."

Soon enough she's there, but has come out a different part than where Billie Jean was. She thinks.

Right?

It's so dark, though.

She unpacks a flashlight, cups her hand over the lens and flicks it on.

It glows harsh for a moment then dies.

She taps it against her other palm but it only sputters light.

"That kind of movie, then," she says. "Car won't start either, will it?"

She's talking because she's nervous.

"But you're not Janet Leigh," she says to herself. "You're not Drew Barrymore. This is completely different, nobody ever sees the slasher during his down time, nobody ever . . . "

Then she senses it, the hulking presence behind her.

"Billie Jean?" she says, wincing because she doesn't want an answer, her hand working the stun gun up from her pocket, and then, at the absolute worst (*best*) possible time

→ that sparkly white glove latches onto her ankle again.

Izzy shrieks exactly like she would crucify herself publicly for doing, and jumps back, into something. Some*body*.

When she turns, she's leading with the stun gun.

It lights the bloody mouthed sheriff up, shocks him back into the water.

He keels over, his grey head crunching into another rock.

Izzy falls back the other way, her hands to her mouth, and, where she's landed, it's right on Billie Jean.

His arms come up around her legs and, like his white hands are spiders, she smashes at them with the stun gun.

It shocks him and her both.

She flops out into the water, goes under, comes up with the sheriff draped around her, his bloody, blubbering face right in hers, his arms hugging her, trying to pull her down.

She screams, and

→ it's loud enough to wake Ben on the couch, for a moment.

He blinks, groggy, drunk, and onscreen, Izzy's left *Slumber Party Massacre* playing, it looks like.

He nods that that was the source of the noise, nods back off.

Back at the creek, Izzy's still screaming, but now she's clapped her own hand over her mouth, is shaking her head no, that this isn't how she's supposed to react.

Her eyes are telling a different story, though.

Slowly, slowly, she controls herself. The sheriff bobbing beside her.

"I'm sorry," she says to him, and pushes him away, trying to use just her palms, not her fingertips.

He rolls in the water like a dead catfish, drifts away.

Izzy treads water for a few moments, actually crying now, her teeth chattering, then she raises the hand still latched onto the stun gun, and stands easily.

She hits the trigger once, nothing, twice, nothing, then, on the third time, it sparks, but the water running off it's still connecting to her.

It gives her a jolt, shorts out, and she throws it away.
The water swallows it, but

→ at that precise moment, that turtle we saw earlier surfaces, as if this stun gun tapped into its shell.

Izzy screams again, even louder, kicks and splashes back, fighting for her life.

Some amount of panic and adrenaline later—it still feels like the same dilated moment—Izzy pulls herself up onto the bank, lies there breathing, breathing. She looks up to her house, and, in

→ her POV, it's still dark.

"Boop, boop, boop," she says, pinching the windows shut with her fingers, some personal game we don't know anything about.

It's enough to steady her for a moment.

Inside the house, the phone rings and rings some more, but nobody's there to answer it. Ben just rolls over, away from the sound, *Slumber Party Massacre* still flickering across the whole living room.

"Shit shit shit," Izzy's saying, staring over to where Billie Jean must be, the panic and truth of all this still hitting her, so that she has to sit down, hug her knees tight.

In her POV, a finger of that white sparkly glove twitches.

Not in her POV, a bloodshot, evil eye opens.

"It wasn't your fault, it wasn't your fault," Izzy's saying to herself now, rocking back and forth. Looking downstream, the scene of the crime slipping away.

"What was he doing down here, anyway? Trespassing? Sneaking up on scantily-clad young girls in the dark? On duty? While *drinking*?"

That reminds her.

She stands, finds her way to the oak, gets the bottle out and takes a long, necessary pull. And then another.

"You killed the sheriff, Izzy," she says to herself, a little drunk already, and not just on the alcohol. She shushes a finger up over her lip, kind of stumbles to one knee.

"Billie Jean," she whispers, "let's, let's tell them it was you, cool?

Not that I wouldn't get some high school cred for taking down the local authority figure, but that's more your thing, right? Anyway, you know, it won't look good on my college apps . . . "

Another long drink.

She holds the bottle out, letting the last swallow slosh in the moonlight.

"Thanks, Dad," she says, about the bottle, and kills it. Then studies Billie Jean's twisted body. His right knee trashed the worst, probably. Or, the one thing obviously wrong.

"I was just being a good Samaritan," Izzy says to the world, unzipping the duffel. "I was—I just came down here to help a fellow . . . a fellow horror fiend, right? The *original* horror fiend. I can't in good conscience deny you aid just because you—well, because you are what you are."

Close on Billie Jean's bloodshot eye, blinking again.
Listening?

"Not much of a talker, are you?" Izzy says to him. "Strong, silent type, let your bodycount do the talking."

No answer.

Izzy cracks the first-aid kit open, finds a penlight in there and clicks it on, the beam red.

She runs it up and down Billie Jean's body, hovers on the leg again.

"You understand of course that doing all this, it gives me a pass on any future carnage, right?"

She pulls out some gauze, some scissors, tries to get them to focus.

"That was a joke," she says to Billie Jean.

Blink. Blink.

"But if you could leave my brat brother out of it too, I guess."

No answer.

"Do you want a burrito or something?" Izzy asks, and

→ we're tight on a burrito in the microwave, bubbling in its paper.

Walking from the kitchen, muddy as she was last time she came through, Izzy stops, takes two steps back, flips a cabinet door open.

What her POV's settled on in there, it's the family pharmacopeia.

Xanax.

Izzy takes it, reads the back of it, looks down to where the creek must be.

"No way," she says, and shoves the bottle back up, reaches over for a box of band-aids instead.

Then she gets a second box as well.

Again she's on her knees, just out of reach of Billie Jean.

She lowers her arm slowly to his, to apply one of these band-aids, but his hand clamps onto hers.

She breaks away easily.

"I'm trying to *help* you," she hisses. "Know what would have happened if you washed up at any of the other stupid houses along here?"

Still, he grabs ineffectually for her.

Izzy backs up, takes a bite of the burrito, easily moves away from his next lunge.

"You might not even be sequel material, really," Izzy says. "Aren't you supposed to heal yourself somehow? That how it works?"

But then he manages to actually grab her.

This time she doesn't jerk away, but lets him hold on.

Slowly, one by one, she peels his fingers up, replaces her arm with the burrito.

He kills it, its guts oozing out.

But then some part of him recognizes it. Smells it maybe.

He pulls it to his face, smears it over his latex mouth.

"I'll take good care of him, Mom," Izzy says, leaning forward to roll the Michael Jackson mask up over Billie Jean's mouth, and her eyes get soft and twelve-years-old for the next part: *"Promise."*

ACT 2

It's a new morning.

We're up above the town establishing, taking stock.

There's school busses, there's men and women with briefcases balancing coffee, there's birds chirping, there's sprinklers, there's the creek purling along, in no particular hurry.

Nothing to suggest the events of last night.

Except maybe the flags at the school. They're still at half mast, and . . . trembling? Has a car bumped into it? Is it an earthquake?

No. It's some long-armed guy monkeying up past the flag, the strap of a backpack clenched in his teeth.

Everybody below's cheering him on.

Well, everybody except Stuart, swiveling his head around for a teacher, a coach, a cop, anybody.

There's just his stupid screaming classmates, though.

"*Go!*" Izzy yells, instead of what we expect: for her to stand up for those who can't stand up for themselves.

It's supposed to be what she's about, right?

She's back in a spare set of glasses, too, that look she manicures that's all about not having a look, the strategic rips in her jeans saying she doesn't care, the hoop in her eyebrow dull and bored with itself.

And then we go close on this guy climbing.

It's Jake.

Of course Izzy's yelling.

An instant later, Jake's big hand grips around that brass ball at the top of the flagpole. He spits the backpack into his other hand, hangs it up on the ball and slides down like a fireman, everybody laughing.

"Jake," Izzy says.

On the ground again, Jake holds his hands up in victory, runs a stupid, self-congratulatory 'I won' Rocky circle, and then, completely out of the blue, he gets clocked in the head by the backpack, sliding down the pole.

Stuart steps forward to claim his bag.

Now Jake's lost face, though.

"Uh-uh," he says, faking a smile, his eyes hot with trouble, and loops an arm through a backpack strap, launches himself the other direction.

Except the other backpack strap's still looped around the pole.

Jake flattens out in the air, comes down hard on his back.

"You really know how to pick them," Brittney says, suddenly standing behind Izzy. "Surprised he's not already in college, I mean."

Izzy looks away.

"As a student, I mean," Brittney adds, handing Izzy her cracked phone, her main glasses. "Not a subject."

Izzy switches glasses, scrolls through her phone: shaky and flickering, there's no calls, about twenty texts. Her fingernail black, a tiny skull decal grinning up through the clearcoat.

She stretches her waist to slide the phone into her pocket, doesn't seem to care about the texts.

"Sorry about last night," she says. "Ditching you with loverboy. How'd that turn out, anyway?"

"You don't know yet, do you?" Brittney says, unable to contain her smile.

"You went home with Clark Kent, didn't you? Was it 'super?' Did he take you to his Fortress, show you his—"

"Come with me," Brittney says, pulling Izzy by the hand, into the

→ school. The crush of bodies, lockers, posters, black crepe paper hanging from the ceiling tile.

"What don't I know?" Izzy's saying, trying to pull away but not really.

"That you're a grade-A *bitch*," Brittney smiles meaningfully, depositing Izzy at a central bulletin board by the main office.

The School Bus Bounce, hand-sized letters just rainbow out "HOMECOMING," though.

"Yeah, official unplanned pregnancy night, but why—?"

"*American Pie . . .* " Brittney says, waiting for Izzy to follow.

"One two, three, or the reunion?" Izzy asks back, squinting.

"I mean *Beauty*. You're the one who made me watch it."

Izzy mouths it, tasting it—*American Beauty, American Beauty*—and finally wows her eyes out, tag-lines it for Brittney: "Look closer . . . "

Brittney bites her bottom lip in, nods too fast, too eager.

Izzy goes back to the homecoming court list, and we go

→ down it name by name with her, in her POV:

LINDSAY BAKER, check.

CRYSTAL BLAKE, okay.

MANDY KANE has the "MANDY" crossed out, replaced with a scratched-in *Kandy*.

And . . . APRIL RIPLEY.

And . . . for that last name we already half-suspect, we go

→ tight on Izzy's eyes. The terror there.

It's a Hitchcock moment, a Marnie shot, zooming in on her, her background falling away. She opens her mouth, can't speak, can only fall back farther

→ all the way to the loud wooden stands of the old gym, the lights off. Class evidently going on already, but not for them.

"Breathe, breathe," Brittney's saying to her.

"It's a joke," Izzy says. "I'm not the right material, I'm—they might put me at zombie prom, I mean, or let me be sweetheart of the woodshop if I give them enough cigarettes, or burn me in effigy at assembly, but—"

"They let her pick her own court," Brittney says, looking away because this part isn't going to go over well. "Since, you know. Last weekend."

"Because of *pity*?"

"Because they all died, Izzy. The whole original court. As in really really dead, not coming back after the credits, April Fool's. The empty seats and single roses at graduation kind of dead, yeah? The get-their-own-page-of-the-yearbook kind of dead. Their parents are all going to divorce and have affairs and wreck their cars now kind of dead. They're not there anymore. And there's not time any more for bids."

"I'm not going to do it," Izzy says. "You didn't think I was, did you?"

Brittney doesn't answer.

"Oh no. No no no," Izzy says, pushing away, the benches slick, pure terror in her eyes.

"Think of what it would do to her if you won."

"It's a set-up, can't you see? She picked girls who—we've . . . girls who worship at the nicotine altar. Girls who don't have just one hair color. Girls who are suspiciously ethnic. Girls who, girls who poke holes in their faces, girls who aren't worried what they're going to look like when they're twenty-five."

"Maybe."

"Maybe?"

"I mean . . . what if she just wants to give everybody a chance, right? What if she's feeling guilty for last weekend?"

"It was Billie Jean who went after her," Izzy says. "Not a fairy godmother."

"You've said it yourself. Slashers make final girls come into their own. Let their inner lights shine."

"I said it like that?"

"You used to believe."

"In horror."

"But everything's horror, isn't it? Sometimes you just can't see the blood."

Izzy swallows, stares high up into the darkness.

"You wish she'd picked you, don't you?" she says to Brittney.

"No, I—" Brittney says, digging in her purse for something.

A cigarette.

"Every girl's dream, right?" Izzy says, leaning forward, elbows on knees.

Brittney's trying to light her cigarette now, failing.

Izzy takes the cigarette, the lighter, breathes it alive. Passes it back.

"I've got a dress you could, you could—if you want," Brittney says, and exhales a mean-girl line of smoke.

Izzy grins a tolerant grin, shakes her head no. Not so much in resistance as in wonder.

"I told you," she says. "Social order's crap this month. Fisherman pulled too many fish out at once. We're all lost in the pond, now. Bumping into each other like, like bumper cars. Trying to figure out who goes where except somebody turned the lights out."

Brittney chuckles.

"What?"

"I thought you were going to keep your metaphors straight this time."

"Do they ask you questions, to win?"

"Questions?"

"Beauty pageant bullshit. 'Do I like starving kids, if I had two wishes, what about the space travel, my stance on masturbation,' all that?"

"Stance?"

"You know what I mean."

"You get to go out at halftime, at the football game," Brittney says, taking another drag. "In front of everybody."

"In front of everybody," Izzy repeats, taking the cigarette from her, getting thoughtful with it. Her fingers are trembling. But there's the ghost of a grin at the corners of her mouth, now.

"So what'd *you* do last night?" Brittney says.

"Later," Izzy says, kind of laughing about *that* particular story. "*Who'd* you do?"

"Slut."

"Whore."

"Got to get it while you can," Izzy shrugs, breathing out smoke, and then jerks her head over to the

→ absolute *crash* of the gym door slamming back, hard enough that its handle powders some of the lacquered brick wall up, lets it hang in that spill of light then rush every direction as

→ Jake spills through the doorway, has to touch the ground with his lead hand to stay balanced.

In his other hand, that damn backpack.

"You get to have an escort, you know," Brittney says as Jake flashes past, seeing them at the last moment, turning sideways to kind of eek his mouth out like he doesn't know what's happening here.

However,

→ doing a cartoon turnaround at the still-open gym door is a male coach, that Ken-doll looking one from before, in the hall. And another just like him, right behind. They've each got whistles cocked up in their mouths, hats pulled low, sunglasses pressed back to their corneas so they're Agent Smiths, pretty much. Except in polyester shorts.

Izzy crushes the cigarette out by her boot, says to Brittney, "Play along here," and then, before Brittney can even register it, Izzy stands, takes a long step out like to flag these coaches down, the bleachers not locked into place because nobody's supposed to be in here.

The bench she puts her foot on, it slides with her foot.

Izzy yelps and throws herself forward, spills out onto the floor right in front of the two huffing coaches, and, just to sell it, she bites down on her lip hard enough to trail a line of blood out, even if she has to spit a couple of times to get the cut primed.

The first coach jumps her neatly and the second slides to an almost-stop, hugging her to keep from crushing her.

When he lets her go, she's holding her knee.

"I think it's, I think it's," she's trying to get out, and we case these coaches, see that, of all things, they're twins.

"She's hurt," Brittney says, swallowing her smile, crashing down to 'help' Izzy. Once there she flashes her eyes through the horizontal empty spaces between the benches, where they fold into each other.

In her POV, there's somebody there, under the stands, watching, reaching forward with a finger to mash out the cherry of the cigarette Izzy didn't quite kill.

It's Jake, the smoke trailing up around his finger. But he holds it there.

Go, Brittney says to him with just her lips, and Izzy convulses under her, in something a lot like pain, except, well, it's really love.

Slow pan on that longsword in the trophy case, kind of catching it from all angles.

Dim in the glass reflection—sunlight all behind, so it's as much shadow as reflection—is a body to attach this POV to, neither male nor female, and so faceless it might as well be wearing a fencing mask, or liquor-store pantyhose.

Still, we get it: somebody's eyeballing that sword.

Thinking certain things.

In an empty hallway, that pigtailed girl who stuck her head in Izzy and Brittney's bathroom earlier, she's walking along with an armful of tests or copies or something. Not particularly happy, not sad, just going from one place to another.

What she can't see behind her, in slow and dramatic motion, is Jake sliding around the corner, pushing off a wall of lockers, running hell for leather up behind her.

"Shit shit shit," he's saying.

Back to that corner he just rounded: those twin coaches, implacable, resolute, not out of breath at all.

One of them—they're running too—hooks his hand on the corner somehow then extends his hand for his brother, who takes his hand rollerball-style, by the wrist, and gets swung around *so* fast, gaining fifteen feet in a heartbeat, easy.

The anchor twin nods about this and backs away. To cut Jake off from another hall, evidently, Jake who's

→ slamming into Pigtails when she unaccountably turns right at the worst possible moment, her papers exploding into the air.

From that mess, Jake slides out, that coach's fingers inches from the back of his shirt now.

"I'm sorry! I'm sorry!" he yells behind him, and, close on his face, we can see that this has gone beyond a prank, now. This is life or death for him. Unlike

→ the ho-humness of two combat boots swinging off the edge of a paper-sheeted bed.

It's Izzy, in the nurse's office.

Brittney's across from her in the waiting chair, the nurse with her back to them, looking through a drawer.

Brittney hisses to Izzy about her carefree feet, makes hot eyes, and Izzy gulps a smile down, pulls her 'hurt' left knee up, to cradle it.

Other, Brittney says with just her lips, and Izzy nods, switches knees just in time.

The nurse turns around.

"Of course we can't put band-aids in your mouth," the nurse says. She's fifty-plus, solid, no nonsense.

"It just hurts," Izzy says, touching her bottom lip.

"Like those?" the nurse says, pointing serially to Izzy's nose ring, her eyebrow hoop, the half-moon of studs through the sensitive part of her left ear.

"What about my knee?" Izzy says. "I want to—I just need to stabilize it, I think. I don't want to miss lab. I think it's pig babies again."

The nurse is so, so bored with Izzy. With high school. With life.

"Crutches?" she says. "You'll have to sign for them."

"I was thinking something more like that," Izzy says, pointing to a diagram on the wall, of a massive knee brace. Like a splint that bends. A serious Robocop leg.

"That's for post-surgery."

"I think I'm pre-surgery right now. If those—if the stands would have just been locked in place . . . "

"In the gym you had written permission to be in?" the nurse adds.

"She has cramps," Brittney blurts out.

The nurse looks back to her, says, "I'm not Principal Masters, you know? That doesn't work on my kind."

"*Our* kind," Brittney corrects.

"It's just—cigarettes help," Izzy says, bringing the fight back to her. "My mom taught me. Something about the nicotine, the vascular . . . "

"Ah, yes. You've got to love modern parenting, don't you?"

"She's what I've got," Izzy says, her voice less needy, now. Something rising in it.

The nurse just stares at her.

"Going for the sympathy vote then, are you?" the nurse says, squatting sideways to dig the large leg brace from under Izzy's table.

"What?"

"*Home*coming votes," Brittney fills in, not amused now either.

"I hear pity's the way to cash in, yeah," Izzy says, trying not to smile.

"You have to sign for this as well," the nurse says, and sets the brace on Izzy's lap.

In Izzy's POV, the brace doesn't look at all like the poster on the wall. All the velcro's matted with hair, there's writing all over it in different hands, and, going by the gagging she's doing, there's a definite smell. Maybe even a stench.

"Is this the—the *boy's* one?" she says, holding it up and away, trying not to touch it.

"Your knee hurts, doesn't it?" the nurse says, satisfied with herself.

Brittney's looking away, trying to keep her lips tight, not letting her eyes catch Izzy's or else they'll collapse with laughter. Cut to

→ the hall outside the main office, Pigtails there with a bloody tissue to her nose, Lindsay there as well, scrolling through her phone, completely bored. She looks up to Izzy, her arm around Brittney's shoulder for support, the brace strapped to her knee.

"What happened?" she says, her voice just dripping with concern.

"I was jumping with joy," Izzy says, cutting a grin down to Lindsay.

"She means thanks for the nomination," Brittney says for Izzy, for which she gets a sharp and secret hair tug from Izzy.

Lindsay doesn't respond, just watches, curious.

"Hop along, now," the nurse says, escorting them

→ through the main office doors, which of course means: she's milking this for all it's worth, is shadowing them just to watch Izzy fake it. To make her *keep* faking it.

And this hall stretching before them, it's forever long.

"I'm going to throw up," Izzy says to Brittney, holding her hand over her nose. From the brace.

"Why'd you even want it?" Brittney says back, turning to make sure the nurse is still watching.

Yep.

"Thank you!" Brittney calls back, so cheerful.

The nurse nods, lifts her face to the hall before Izzy and Brittney:

It's Jake, sweaty-faced, racing, that guilty backpack hooked over his shoulder.

Nobody behind him now, either.

He slows by Izzy and Brittney, slides to both knees so that his fingertips stop at Izzy's brace.

He looks up to her about it.

"Me?" he says, wincing in apology.

"Flesh wound," Izzy says, rotating her foot to show how whole she is.

"Speaking of," Brittney chimes in, up on her tiptoes beside them.

They both look to her, lost.

"Speaking of flesh wounds?" Izzy asks.

"Of words that start with F," Brittney says. "Like . . . Friday, football game, *frome*coming . . ."

"Britt, we didn't—"

"That's right," Jake fills in, leaning down to catch Izzy's eyes. "Tomorrow, right?"

She lets him look. Looks back.

"Interested?" she says. "I'll make you *famous*."

His nod goes from slight to grinning, and it spreads to Izzy, and Brittney just amplifies it.

"You had me at F," he says, "pick you up at—?" but doesn't get to finish.

Something's rattling around the corner.

Jake goes up onto the balls of his feet, ready to explode off in twenty directions at once, but then that last hall before the main doors, where the sound's coming from—it's just a lab cart. Fourteen or sixteen jars of pig babies, Stuart pushing them.

"*Stu-baby!*" Jake says, and Stuart looks from Jake to Izzy to the backpack, and then behind them, to

→ one of the twin coaches, just walking. But with purpose. With Terminator intent.

Izzy hauls Jake to her other side, her safe side, says on the way, "It's okay, we'll talk, just go," and pushes him towards the exit.

"Miss Stratford?" the nurse says, nodding down to the leg Izzy's most definitely standing on.

Izzy doesn't let any expression show, just says it again, to Jake: "*Go.*"

"Seven o'clock?" Jake says, starting to gather himself, and Izzy nods, bites her bloody lower lip in pure pleasure.

Jake smiles back, thanking her with his eyes, and turns to run for the double doors, has to pull up short when the other twin coach steps out from behind the trophy case.

"Jacob Jacob Jacob . . . " the coach says.

"Don't call me that," Jake says, backpedaling, bumping into the abandoned pig baby cart.

He commandeers it, rolls it towards the coach coming up the hall.

That coach catches it, stops.

"This is going to suck," Brittney says, both her hands clamped on Izzy, to keep her from doing anything stupid.

Still, love is what it is.

Izzy takes a step forward and fakes her braced knee collapsing, falls in a pile on the floor before the pig baby cart.

"My leg!" she says, reaching up for help, her voice shrieky and perfect, Lindsay framed in the wire-mesh glass behind her, just watching this develop.

"Ms. Stratford," the nurse tsk-tsks.

"I didn't even—here," Jake says, tossing the backpack to Stuart, showing that this can all just be over.

Stuart tosses it back, timidly.

Jake cocks his head, lost, and looks to the coaches for help.

"He just . . . we're friends," Jake says, obviously making it up as he goes, tossing the bag to Stuart again, who tosses it *back* again.

Jake smiles. "See?" he says. "We've known each other since, since third grade, right, Stu old buddy?"

"Go to hell," Stuart says, an evil grin spreading on his face.

"What?" Jake says, "I was just—"

"Jacob," the trophy-case coach says.

"*Don't call me that!*" Jake screams, pissed off now, and stabs his hand into the bag. "Listen, I just, I was just, I wanted to borrow a book from Stu, okay? I just wanted to borrow this, this . . . "

What he pulls up, though, it isn't a book.

It's a semi-automatic pistol.

Jake opens his mouth in shock, and looks up to the hall coach, then into the main office, all the people in there diving behind the counter. Except Lindsay. For whom this just became interesting.

Moments later the fire alarm screams, the lights go dim, emergency flashers strobe the institutional tile.

"No," Jake says like a question, and looks up to

→ the hall coach, who's footballed up a pig baby jar, is rolling it in his hand, feeling for the stitches.

"Jacob Stadler!" the trophy-case coach calls out, turning Jake's head that way for just long enough.

"Noooo!" Izzy yells, reaching up into the air above her head, but it's too late, the

→ pig baby jar is already spiraling along a laser line in slow-motion, practically breaking the sound barrier, and

→ we go around and around it, tracing its spiral, tight on that pig baby's mouth, locked forever in a

→ scream, from Izzy;

→ an appreciative grin, from Lindsay.

Brittney looks away so she doesn't have to see the jar catch up to real speed, *slam* into Jake's shoulder, spinning him around, the gun coming up, his hand twitching around it to hold on, so that one shot fires up into the ceiling, sifting white dust down around him.

He looks down to the pistol like he wants to shake it off his finger, and then the next jar catches him. In the face. And it's ugly enough that we cut ahead, to

→ the parking lot, everybody who was in the school standing out there holding each other, adopting the various postures of grief they know so well from television.

News trucks, police cars. A helicopter blowing Izzy's hair down into her eyes, so she has to clear it in order to tighten her POV down to Deputy Dante, the one in charge here.

"Shit on a stick," Izzy says.

"What?" Brittney says.

An ambulance gurney wheels out, Jake's face wrapped in bandages, and Izzy digs her fingers into Brittney's arm.

"That flag go any lower?" Izzy says, faking a smile, her thick eyeliner all smeared up.

Brittney pulls her closer.

"Somebody needs to do something about this place," Izzy says.

Brittney looks over to the top of Izzy's head, concerned.

"I think that was kind of Stuart's idea," she says, both of them watching as Stuart is led out in handcuffs, Dante pushing him each time he tries to just scuffle along.

"You working this afternoon?" Izzy asks.

"I don't think anybody's going to be plundering the video shelf," Brittney says. "I'll just check in . . . anyway, we've got to go give statements, right? Eyewitnesses, baby doll, front and center. Why?"

"Got something to show you," Izzy says meaningfully, no grin to her voice now. She threads a clump of purple-streaked bangs out of her face, and we shuttle ahead, to

→ Izzy and Brittney through the back window of a Sheriff's car, that car pulling them out of the parking lot.

We go with, are facing them in the backseat.

"That your mom?" Izzy says, about Brittney's vibrating phone.

Brittney flips it open, says, "Dad. He's more the news hound."

Izzy nods. Is happy for her. Busies herself velcroing and unvelcroing the top strap of her leg brace.

"You ever feel like you're in the prequel, like?" Izzy says to Brittney. "Like the important stuff, the stuff that really matters, it's just next, after this?"

"It's called high school," Brittney says back without having to think about it, flashing her eyes at the woman deputy behind the wheel, that deputy narrowing her eyes in concern but not butting in.

"If we survive," Izzy says,

→ and then that woman deputy is guiding them through the mobbed Sheriff's headquarters, a place *not* built for this kind of attention. Guiding them through, through, to

→ a central office, Deputy Dante rising to greet them. He's huge, as always, and twice as imposing as usual.

Izzy swallows, tightens her lips.

"I didn't do it," she blurts out anyway.

Deputy Dante guides them down to the two perp chairs, their arms chewed with fingernails.

"Now that we've got that out of the way," he says, taking a seat himself.

"This is Sheriff Mills' office," Brittney says, looking around at

→ the name plaque;

→ a fishing picture;

→ a nudie calendar, woefully out of date, two googley eyes on the calendar girl like pasties.

Dante shrugs Brittney's observation off, looks pointedly to Izzy for this question: "Were you expecting him?"

"He was at our house last night," Izzy says too fast, licking her lips as well. Digging her fingers into the arm of the chair.

Dante looks from Izzy to Brittney, wheels turning behind his eyes.

"You hurt your leg?" he says to Izzy.

"It's fake," Izzy says. "Oh, wait, no. I hurt it while killing the sheriff, yes."

"Go on," Dante says.

"He was at your house?" Brittney says, turning to see Izzy.

"Our street," Izzy says. "Door to door, something about masks, I don't know. From the Lindsay thing, right?"

Dante doesn't answer, just adjusts his toothpick. Today it's bright yellow, hard to miss.

"I thought we were here for Jake," Brittney says. "It was a complete set-up. Stuart tricked him. Revenge of the nerds, all that."

Dante's just boring his eyes into Izzy.

"You two wouldn't have been up on the point last night about dusk, would you have?" he finally says.

"Memorial service," Izzy says, but we can hear the gamble in her voice.

"Thought so," Dante says, sliding today's paper across to them, "LINDSAY'S RIDE" the sixty-point headline.

Just under it and to the right is a photo of the Billie Jean mask, backdropped by the cliff, all that open space.

The only other thing in the photo is a female wrist, bangled with black bracelets.

The same ones Izzy's still wearing.

"Like we told *him*," Izzy says, pushing the paper back. "We grieve in our own way."

"Of course you do. And keep the paper. I've got plenty."

"What about Jake?" Brittney says again.

"Stupid is as stupid does," Dante says.

"I want to talk to the real sheriff," Brittney says. "My dad knows him."

"Mine too," Izzy says, but weaker.

"I bet you would like to talk to him," Dante says again, straight at Izzy.

"What the hell?" she says back, standing now.

Dante shakes his head no, nothing, but can't help smiling about her reaction.

"Guess I don't need anything else," he says, standing as well, raising his arm to usher them out.

"That's it?" Brittney says, incredulous.

"I'll just take you out the—" Dante says, sliding through the people, pulling Brittney and Izzy along, "out the other way," but it's *so* not an accident:

→ there, in an office, in Izzy's slow-motion, sliding POV, that kind of 'surprise reunion' shot of two people passing in cars going opposite ways kind of feel, it's Crystal Blake, sitting under a serene picture of an abandoned lakeside camp.

Izzy stops, never sees Dante's satisfied grin.

It's gone by the time he comes back around, his surly face back on.

"What's she doing here?" Izzy says. "She wasn't even at school this morning, she couldn't have seen anything."

"You know she wasn't there?" Dante asks.

"I was going to tell her she was on the list."

"The list?"

"Of homecoming losers."

Dante nods, as if seeing Crystal for the first time all over again. As homecoming material. But then he shrugs it off. Says, "She—it doesn't concern the Jacob thing. That's all you need to know."

"It's Jake," Izzy corrects.

And, in her POV, looking closer: has Crystal been crying?

Her, crying?

"Come on," Brittney says, tugging Izzy's hand.

Izzy pulls free, steps up to the glass between her and Crystal.

"She's been through enough already," Izzy says, turning hard on Dante. "What are you holding her on? Smoking in the ladies room? Skirt's not past her fingertips?"—Brittney trying to pull Izzy away, out of this—"You don't have any bigger fish to fry today, Deputy?"

Dante chuckles about all this. "Of course I can't speak—"

"Bull. Fucking. Shit," Izzy says.

This stops Dante's chuckle. His toothpick goes rigid.

"My dad'll call Sheriff Mills," Brittney says, tugging Izzy as away as she can.

"Must have some goddamn phone, then," Dante says back to Brittney, but looking at Izzy.

"What did she do?" Izzy says again, actually kind of pleading now.

"We're not announcing anything yet," Dante says. "Enough news for one day already."

"You can't hold her," Izzy says. "She didn't do anything."

"And how would you know that?" Dante says, flicking his eyes behind Izzy, for Izzy to look.

It's Crystal at the window, all that painted water framing her.

"Just leave," she says, and she *has* been crying. But now she's not. And, judging by how firm her lips are, she won't be again, either. Not today.

Izzy Spocks her hand up to the glass but Brittney's already pulling her out of this scene.

Next, or now, or later, a predatory POV is stalking up the sterile hallway of a hospital.

It looks down at a tray of surgery gear on a paper mat.

Then a wall of names, blinking like arrivals and departures.

Then away from a nurse, who recognizes whoever this is, is wowing her eyes out, stepping aside.

And looking away from the next nurse as well.

Step, step, until a big arrangement of flowers pushes open the door of one of these rooms, and we know shotguns fit so perfectly in roses, and the music's low key enough we can hear that distinctive breathing, and there's the occupant of the room, half his face bandaged, startling over to whoever this is, but

→ reversing, it's only Lindsay, in her sling, barely able to manage these flowers.

"Are you all right?" she says ever so earnestly, settling the vase onto his food tray, and we go

→ close on the note strung around the neck of that classy vase: JACOB. With a heart and a smiley face.

"What are you doing here?" Jake asks, and the handwriting on that note we're still close on blurs

→ shivers back as "REASON FOR ABSENCE."

As we watch, a feathered-up pen slashes through that blank, fills in *stupid fucking people*, and we flip around, to see who this is.

Izzy and Brittney, of course. Izzy with the pen.

The front counter of the main office of Danforth High.

Izzy jams the pen down for a period, the pink boa feather taped to it shuddering.

"Well," Marty the secretary says, collecting the pen, flipping it slowly to study the impacted ball. Dabbing it on the pad of her finger to be sure.

"Want me to just go on in?" Izzy says, holding her hand open to Principal Masters' office, the knob naked now. "Looks like he's . . .

how do you say it? Unoccupied, yeah."

"It's fifth period," Marty says back primly, no eye contact, and Brittney pulls Izzy away again, this time to

→ the girls' locker room.

Of course.

All kinds of girls walking around in towels, never quite showing anything but all those near misses seemingly just bad luck, not choreography.

Izzy's sitting there watching them through the steam, Brittney rummaging in a locker beside her.

"They're all asking for it," Izzy says, about the naked girls moving through the steam.

"You're in here too," Brittney says back.

"Misfit never dies until late," Izzy recites, undoing the top strap of her knee brace. "Then they get to go out doing something heroic. Recuperate themselves right at the end. Makes you re-evaluate all those burners in the halls on Monday."

"You want to be an Air Force Ranger, don't you?"

"He won't even remember," Izzy says, looking up to Brittney. "About tomorrow night, I mean."

"Got to admit, though," Brittney says, peeling out of her shirt but we're at face-level with Izzy, slouching on the bench, "it's a great origin story. Think he'll come back as . . . what? Butcher Boy? Pig Face? Just, instead of camp counselors, he's out for coaches. Each practice there's another mysterious, sports-themed accident . . . "

"And nobody recognizes him . . . " Izzy fills in, playing along.

"You can ask somebody else, you know?" Brittney says, coming down to Izzy's level on the bench to tie her shoes but her bare back's to us.

"I'm not even going to go," Izzy says. "It was stupid. A little girl's princess dream."

"What about Crystal?"

Izzy looks over to Brittney. "What do you mean?"

"What if this is *her* secret dream, but under that tough girl exterior she'd never in a million years have the balls to glam up in front of a cheering crowd of public nacho eaters?"

"Never?"

"I mean, not without some other reject to stand up there with her. Hold her hand."

"You suck."

"That's what they say."

"Dante's got her for something anyway."

Brittney slithers into her gym tank top, stands again to pull it down.

"Nacho eaters?" Izzy says at last, finally getting the brace off.

"*Public* nacho eaters," Brittney corrects. "I mean, we all do it in private, right?"

"I've got to get some new friends," Izzy says, smiling with half her mouth.

"Hitting English today?" Brittney asks, ready to slope out to the floor, the gym, the track, whatever torture's cued up for them. "We're getting papers back, right?"

Izzy winces, shuts her eyes.

Meanwhile, back at the ranch, Ben and the leaf boy are playing some hooky. Strolling downhill behind the homestead, each of them trailing one of Jamie's cigarettes, leaf boy watery-eyed and coughing from his.

They're taking those long cartoon steps you do when on this steep a place.

Long and careless steps.

We go ahead of them, to where Billie Jean should be.

Nothing?

"I know she keeps one here somewhere," Ben says. We can just see his face past his hand, his arm stabbed deep into the tree.

This is the vodka's POV.

Ben brushes it, tips it . . .

→ pulls it up into the open air like a sacred golden statue.

Meaning this is that moment before that boulder starts rolling.

Ben sloshes the nothing in there, twists the top off, turns the bottle up all the same, just on principle.

"You hear something?" leaf boy's asking, half-behind Ben, while half-behind *him*, there's all this open space, each leaf crisp, because that's where we're already focusing.

And—is that background kind of shuffling? Are those leaves waking up?

"You should see it when her friend Britt comes over," Ben says, turning the bottle upside down to show how it's even more empty now.

"What do you mean?" leaf boy says, unaccountably nervous.

"She's the one who works at the video store," Ben says, stepping across exactly where Billie Jean should be—

Yes?

—and squatting down to the creek, tilting the bottle in, letting the water gurgle in.

Behind him, nothing in a mask rises.

But we're waiting.

"Ms. Glynnis going to notice we're not there, you think?" leaf boy says.

Ben stands, caps the bottle, steps across those leaves *again* to get back to the tree.

"I'll say my sister knew some of those dead kids," Ben shrugs, cramming the bottle back in its place. "And, if you know me, then you kind of know her too, right? And then you know them as well, are in mourning." He shrugs, looking around, taking his cigarette from behind his ear. "We're at the cemetery or somewhere right now," he shrugs. "Don't worry. We're gone, man, evaporated."

As illustration, he poofs the ash up from his cigarette, which

→ we stay with, still listening to them, down below somewhere.

"Speaking of," leaf boy says. "Who ate all your burritos?"

While we're smiling from that, our defenses down, that poof of ash blurs into

→ a chalkboard, somebody erasing up there.

Reversing onto the classroom, it's just high school kids grimacing about graded papers, but of course we single out Brittney at her desk, texting.

The books on the desk tell us this is English.

The empty desk in front of Brittney tells us that Izzy's

→ in the hall with the English teacher, who looks like he should be at a bar, or on WKRP in Cincinnati, the unreformed stoner.

"But Mr. Pleasance," Izzy's saying, one shoulder cocked up on the wall, her eyes darting from locker to locker to janitor, the paper she just got back clenched by her thigh.

"It's not the quality of the writing or the level of thought involved, Izzy, it's, it's—"

"How can it be poor taste if I turned it in before they traipsed off into the woods with targets on their backs?"

"I'm just saying. You need something for your college portfolio. And so far all you've got are meditations on different aspects of horror movies. Kill ratios don't get you into the Ivy League, you know that, right? And breast count, that's been done. Though your hypothesis about how older-model ignition circuits must have been baked into the side windows of certain cars, that's inventive, no doubt, but you want to lead with your best foot."

They both look down to her ragged combat boots.

"Let me put it another way," Mr. Pleasance says, crossing his arms because he's shifting up to 'serious' and 'helpful' now. "Do you want to get out of here?"

"You can't imagine."

"Then make Jane Austen your friend."

"Frankenstein?"

"Dickens."

"God. Prick me, do I not bleed?"

"Good, good, more like that."

"I saw it in a Ron Jeremy movie," Izzy says, still watching that janitor, who seems to be mopping just the same place over and over. Listening in? "Something about virgins, I think."

From inside the classroom, then, a scream like somebody just woke from a nightmare.

"Speaking of," Izzy says, pulling the door open,

→ Brittney practically hovering in her plastic seat.

"Brittney?" Mr. Pleasance says, adopting his casual stance against the desk.

"Sorry, sorry," she says, stuffing her phone under her thigh, the rest of her still perky and misdirecting. "I just, I never got a B before!"

"You earned a *C*," Mr. Pleasance says, his tone all about defeat. "Again."

"I bet *she'd* go a D . . . " a wannabe Jake says from the back of the classroom. "Couple of them."

"Mr. Davis," Mr. Pleasance says, disappointed, and angles his head at the door.

Davis stands, collects his books, says, "It was worth it," then, in passing, to Brittney: "Tomorrow night?"

"That would be homecoming," Brittney says.

"She's spoken for," Izzy says, daring Davis to call her on this.

"I see," he says, waggling his eyebrows about Izzy and Brittney.

"You wish," Izzy says.

"*People*," Mr. Pleasance says.

"More like we all know," Davis says back, shooting them both with imaginary sex pistols.

"And that matters how?" Brittney throws in.

"People, people," Mr. Pleasance is still saying.

It finally works.

The door closes behind Davis and Izzy slides into her desk, slouched back far enough to whisper to Brittney, "*You screamed?*"

"My knight in torn pantyhose," Brittney says.

"Don't forget the metal armor," Izzy smiles back, waggling her studded tongue.

"Ladies," Mr. Pleasance is saying now, breathing deep for the king of all massive sighs.

"Right you are," Izzy says, fingershooting *him* now.

"Cell, cell," Brittney hisses, her eyes hot from all the attention.

Izzy slides lower in her seat, works her phone up from her boot. Has to shake it to get it to flicker on.

"Stupid horror movie phones," she says to herself, and we see Britt's message pop on its shattered screen, but instead of reading it with Izzy, we swing around for her response.

This class has just gone from the usual bull session to deadly serious.

Izzy looks back to Brittney to be sure.

Brittney bites her lip, nods once, as if fearful of Izzy's response.

"Izzy?" Mr. Pleasance asks, his sigh infecting his eyes, now. His face.

"I, um, is Jane Austen in the library?" Izzy says politely, standing with her bag and waiting expectantly.

Mr. Pleasance stares at her. And stares at her.

"And, you have a sudden interest in the literature of manners as well, Brittney?" he says.

"Which way *is* the library?" Brittney says back, wheeling her eyes all around the school, and

→ we're there, Van Santing smoothly and silently up the deserted halls, as if moving towards some big thing, some event:

It's Izzy and Brittney, in the girl's bathroom again, passing a cigarette back and forth at high velocity, their eyes furtive, fingers nervous.

It's still high-stakes land, yeah.

"I should have told him my dad *used* to know the sheriff," Brittney says, exhaling in the general direction of stall two, even though the window's not open there.

"Dante would have thought you did it then," Izzy says, gripping each side of the sink, staring into the mirror. "Cops love to trip you up like that."

"Crystal was right there when they found him, though. Like, poking him with a stick or something."

"Which is exactly what you do when you're guilty of murder. That bridge is between her house and here. She just saw him, probably thought he was a blow-up doll or something."

"A *really* blown-up doll," Brittney says, trying not to smile, trying not to release all this tension.

We already know what they're talking all around, though: Crystal Blake's up for the sheriff's death. And Izzy's feeling the weight of that, the guilt of that.

"Ladies love a man in uniform," she says, angling over to the stall, knocking them lightly open one by one. "I don't think her file's going to help her either," she says.

"Oh, the file—" Brittney says, trying to look back in time. Not seeing anything, evidently.

"Another mark against her, then," Izzy says, as if this is really no surprise. "They'll say she took it because it was too incriminating. Meaning they'll have to go off whatever Mrs. Graves can remember from it. And *that's* going to be worse than what's really there. *Shit.*"

She slams the last door shut.

It bounces back slowly, the hinges creaking.

"But what if she *did* do it?" Brittney asks, waving the smoke away from her face.

"She didn't."

"She could have. Not like she doesn't have an issue or two to work through."

"It wasn't her."

"He just fell in by himself?"

"He was drinking when he came by our place," Izzy says, stepping into stall two to cock the window open.

"Why do you care?" Brittney says, their cigarette very Parisian and casual in her hand suddenly, like a pose she's practicing, leaning up against the sink, her cowboy boots crossed.

"Because it could be me down there, going through that legal meat grinder."

"If you're innocent, then why not, right? More exciting than this place. She's probably milking it, I mean. Crossing her legs like a superstar."

Izzy doesn't answer this. She's reading the graffiti Crystal left:

Inset, Crystal's *slashers that aren't?* has been answered in pencil:
Glenn Close
T-1000
Alien

"Hunh," Izzy says, touching the penciled names, as if for communion. "You do this?"

"I never use that one," Brittney says. "That's a step, not a toilet. Why?"

"Somebody got it right," Izzy says. "There's another horror fan roaming these halls . . . "

→ and again, we're swooping and diving slowly along the lockers, finally crashing towards the front doors, so that

→ "Jailbreak," feels right, when Izzy says it.

"What?" Brittney says, doing her lips in the mirror now, fumbling her lipstick to the floor.

"We need to bust her out. Crystal."

"Oh, that," Lindsay says, picking up her now-grody lipstick. "You Thin Lizzy, or me? And does 'thin' mean that athletic kind of slender, or's it more like 'oh this meth is good do you have some more' kind of skinny?"

"It's the internet age," Izzy says, pushing decisively away from the sink.

Brittney runs her lipstick under the tap but finally just gives up, drops it in the sink, all that red swirling the drain, which we get but are tired of already.

"Don't wait for me!" Brittney calls after Izzy, then stops to pop her lips in the mirror before stepping away, to

→ Izzy's upper-level locker.

"Seriously?" Izzy says, stepping aside so Brittney can see the dated school photo of her taped to the locker, framed in a magnetic princess tiara.

No, a *homecoming* crown.

"One day left to vote . . . " Brittney sing-songs.

Izzy shakes her head, swings the locker open and it's a pack rat nest, that nasty knee brace threatening to spill out onto them. Izzy closes her eyes to shove her hand in, dig, dig—"Remember when we were doing this?" she says, baring her teeth with strain—and finally gives birth to the microphone part of an old CB, just . . . without the spirally cord?

Except that doesn't go with the look of success on Izzy's face.

She raises it ominously to her mouth, says, "*And then there were none*" through it. It's a voice changer, a good one, makes her male and creepy, not herself at all.

"You still have yours?" Brittney says, excited that these are still in the world.

"*She didn't do it, Deputy,*" Izzy adds, disregarding Brittney. "*I did. And this is just the beginning . . .* "

"Dante'll never buy it."

"Crystal's dad's a lawyer, right?" Izzy says, then holds the voice-changer up: "Submitted for your approval. Reasonable doubt 101."

"You seriously suck with metaphors, girl."

Izzy shuts her locker and

→ they're already standing at the payphone in the courtyard, Brittney holding the frayed metal cord out as if trying to understand how this fits with their plans.

It doesn't.

"Oh, oh yeah," Brittney says, eeking her mouth out in pre-apology, holding the frayed cord up as evidence. "Jake was talking on the talking part in Calculus the other day. He was trying to see if Mr. Grant would take it up, put it in the contraband drawer. I was wondering where he got it, like, the antique store, right? I forget about this, though. Weird."

"And we can't use our own phones," Izzy's saying, stepping away to look around.

"Excuse me? I was talking about Jake, you know? *Jake*-Jake? Dreamboat Jake? 'Yeah, *you*'-Jake?"

"We can't use our own phones to place this particular call," Izzy says, holding up the voice-changer. "And I think Marty at the front desk'll notice if we, you know, use a Darth Vader voice at the phone by her desk."

Brittney shrugs, takes the voice-changer, and, pulling her V'd fingers sideways across her eyes, gives us a little "*Dearly beloved, we are gathered here today to get through this thing called life, life, life.*"

Izzy gives her a humorless look.

"We can't save her if we can't call," Izzy says, thinking aloud. "And, and we can't call without Dante knowing it's us. Shit. I *hate* the internet age. How are you supposed to get anything done? What about the days when you had to call the operator to see who was calling, and she had to look it up for like twenty minutes?"

"Oh, you mean those days before you were born?"

Izzy glares at her.

"*Dearly beloved*," Brittney says right directly to her, through the rig again, trying to get that explicit creak down just right.

Izzy takes the voice-changer away from her.

"*Think*," she says. "What phone is there here at Slaughter High that's clean enough to call the cops?"

" . . . *ain't gonna let the elevator break, us, down*," Brittney answers, changing her own voice now.

"You're not helping."

Brittney shrugs, pops her gum, studies this courtyard they're in, her POV settling on that janitor Izzy was watching earlier, guiding his mop bucket through some double doors, into the school.

"Teacher's lounge?" Brittney tries, walking the halls with Izzy. "Cafeteria? Master Bates there"—the janitor—"he probably finds a few phones mixed in with the tampons and condoms."

"He's not a Chester, I don't think. I think he's like a, a Cropsy in waiting, just add fire."

"You love him a little, don't you? It's the sweater, isn't it?"

Izzy flashes her eyes across at Brittney like Brittney's touched a nerve. "Cropsy's the underdog. They all are. Just getting back what's theirs. With interest. In blood. Have I taught you nothing?"

"Shh, shh," Brittney says to all the children not in attendance around Izzy. "Randy's about to go off."

"It's what Billie Jean's doing too."

"Watch your tenses there, missy. What'd they do to him to deserve all that killage, then?"

"I don't know. But unicorn girl does."

" . . . Lindsay? Thought she rode a horse or something? Or is this phallic again? Everything's phallic, right?" As they pass a locker with a large penis carved in it. "Especially high school."

"Unicorn as in 'pure.' It's something I wrote for Donald Pleasance—"

"He hates it when you call him that."

"—it's how golden age slashers were all basically marching orders for would-be princesses. 'Be good,' 'stay chaste,' 'study hard.' Or die the ugliest death Tom Savini can dream up. I used to think that's why my dad was making me watch them all. Because he didn't know how to talk to a girl, but still had hopes, you know?"

"And?"

"I paid attention to all the wrong parts, I guess," Izzy smiles, taking them

→ around a corner, right into one of the twin coaches, splashing his coffee up into the air. Athletic dude that this coach is, he slithers away from the mess.

Still: oops.

This coach appraises them individually, not stepping aside yet.

"You didn't have to do that to Jake's face," Izzy says. "It was kind of overkill, don't you think?"

"He had a gun, Mrs. Spiccoli."

"Oh, you're funny too? Full package, right? Of double-mint?" She lets that settle. "It wasn't *his* gun."

"I didn't look for a nametag, I just reacted."

"Flying pork attack, three o'clock," Brittney chimes in.

"It's not as bad as it looked, either," the coach says, stretching his neck a bit to look behind them at something very very interesting. Neither of them fall for it. "You gave your statements already?" he says.

"'It was police brutality, Officer,'" Izzy recites.

"*Coach* brutality, Coach," Brittney adds, kind of taking the punch out of it.

"He'll be back sooner than you think," the coach says, making motions to get out of this little tribunal.

"Happening a lot around here," Izzy says, and the coach eyeballs her about this but doesn't ask, just steps aside.

A few steps past, Brittney turns halfway around, waving: "Mr. Wrigley, Mr. Wrigley!"

The coach stops, absorbing this blow, and says, without turning around, "It's Winkle."

"*When* will he back?" Izzy says.

"Sooner than we think, right?" Brittney answers, her voice so cheery.

The coach is already walking away again, balancing his coffee high.

"Twins," Izzy spits, coming back around to their walking talk.

"Always ganging up on you," Brittney agrees. "I mean, present company excluded."

"I don't think you're a twin anymore if your brother's dead."

"Maybe we can call from his phone," Brittney says, turning around to make sure the coach isn't right there, but

→ in her POV, he *is!*

Except it's not him. His brother.

We can tell by the clipboard he's managing.

"Coach, coach," Izzy and Brittney say, doing a double take, barely containing themselves until he's gone.

"You think he heard?"

"It wouldn't be fair to use their phone," Izzy says. "Even if they do deserve it."

"What, calling from their office would be a low blow?"

"Dante's coming for whoever he connects the call to. Where would that put us in the karmic cycle, then?"

"Oh, Miss Boy Scout." Knock-knocking on Izzy's head, speaking up into her ear. "Excuse me, is Evil Izzy still in there?"

"It's not about that," Izzy says, brushing Brittney off. "It's about survival. You do something cheap like that in a slasher, you pay for it in blood in the third reel."

"And this is *so* a slasher, right? Thought that part was over already."

"Slashers are never over. That's just what they want you to think."

"Then what were you telling Jamie last night?"

"You already just call him 'Jamie?' Does he know that?"

"What about Pleasance, then? His phone, it's always right there. He gave me a C."

"Does this matter to you at all?" Izzy asks.

"It's Crystal," Brittney shrugs. "For all we know, she did it, I mean. I don't think anybody'd put it past her."

"Not her style," Izzy interrupts, their walk having taken them full-circle enough that they're seeing the janitor again.

He looks up as if aware she's watching him.

They pass, pass, Brittney holding onto Izzy's arm, kind of skirting this janitor now.

"This isn't a slasher," Brittney says to Izzy, now. "You have to have dead teens everywhere for that. Not one old dead sheriff drowned in three feet of water. Anyway, Lindsay's not ready for round two yet. She hasn't had enough time to get some new issues."

"Good point. Next installment's college, likely. Whole new group of sacrifices, change of location, up the ante . . . unless the hook this time, for us, is that Billie Jean didn't really die, right? Then pretend the credits never even rolled. *Halloween II*. Immediate continuation."

"Other way, other way," Brittney says, guiding Izzy through a random door when her POV catches Mr. Pleasance on the approach, reading a student paper as he walks, looking up a sliver of a moment too late for his POV to be sure that's Izzy or Brittney.

However, where Brittney's escaped them to, that door she picked because it was closest, it opens onto the *library*.

"Shh," the librarian says from her station.

Brittney and Izzy look around at this brave new world, then nod to Mr. Pleasance, passing by: *we're here like we said*.

"Go on, say it," Brittney says. "I saved our fine asses."

"I've been here . . . " Izzy says, nodding to herself, cataloging the shelves, the carrels, the tables. "Linda the Barbarian," she says, about the librarian, "and," pointing with her finger to the unmanned reference desk, "and . . . "

Brittney shivers, looking at all these shelves, all these books.

"Stuart," Izzy says then. "*Stuart* works here."

"Work*ed*," Brittney corrects. "Maybe there's a book here about tenses, think?"

"That's it," Izzy says, clutching Brittney into the closest empty aisle. "Dante's already got him, so it *couldn't* be him calling."

"Shh," the librarian says, somehow standing in the aisle with them now.

Izzy and Brittney startle into each other, push away slowly.

"What, is she a ninja?" Brittney whispers.

"I told you, barbarian," Izzy says, and pulls Brittney into a study carrel, walking backwards with her finger across her lips for the librarian.

"*Stuart*," Izzy says again, her face close to Brittney's.

Brittney's popping her head up, meerkatting around for the librarian.

Izzy pulls her back down.

"And Stuart, he's *actually* guilty," Izzy adds, so excited by this.

"I know, I know!" Brittney fakes. "He almost shot the whole school up, right? We were *so* close to being famous . . ."

"Shh," Izzy says, pulling her chin closer to the table top. "I'm saying we use his phone to spring Crystal."

"That would be perfect, yes," Brittney says. "I mean, can we Bill & Ted back in time, borrow it from him, or should I warm up the DeLorean?"

"Think I can do better than that," Izzy says, standing, scanning, scanning

→ her POV settling on that pigtailed girl we've been seeing. She's important after all.

"Hey, April," Izzy calls, forgetting where she is for a moment.

"Shh," everybody says to her.

Izzy and Brittney crash April's private little study party. There's still tissue shoved up her nose, from the impact with Jake.

"April," Izzy says, leaning conspiratorially across the table.

"Do I know you?" April whispers, leaning away, keeping an eye on Brittney as well.

"You told us about Lindsay coming back," Brittney says. "Thank you! Isn't it wonderful?"

"Yes?" April says, her finger still in her book like she can click her heels, go back to that place.

Izzy takes both her hands in hers, though.

"We're sisters now," Izzy says.

"Oh, yeah," April says. "You mean because neither of us rate on the social scale? Or is it that we've dated all the same boys? Or our fashion decisions? Our hair styles? Our grades, our future plans? Do I want to be a full-time skank too when I grow up? You're right, I *do*. Gosh, you're right. Thank you, thank you. Do you want to get matching bracelets now, or share make-up? BFFs, right? Or does that stand for what it actually sounds like?"

And she gives Izzy's hands a meaningful squeeze.

Izzy takes her hands back calmly. Has to work her lips to keep from snapping back.

"You thought this was going to be easy, didn't you?" April says.

"I don't even know what this is," Brittney says, watching the librarian watch her back.

"So what do you need?" April says. "Is this course-work related, or does it involve files from the office? Files cost more."

"We need to get into the biology lab," Izzy says.

April twitches her eyes, doing the mental calculations necessary to say "Sixth period is AP. Can't you just wait?"

"Pretend we can't," Izzy says.

"Shh," the librarian says in passing, rapping her knuckles on their tabletop, daggering her eyes to all three girls.

"Shhh-*what?*" Izzy says, at full voice, rapping her knuckles on the table as well. "Shhhrink my ass to fit in this dress again, like ten years ago? Shhhrooms are good for you? Shhhrodinger's cat is dead?"

Brittney looks away, ovals her mouth out not to smile, and Izzy just glares up at the librarian.

"What do you think is the worst thing I can say to you, dear?" the librarian asks.

"'Shhhower with me?'"

"You remind me of another seventeen-year-old girl I used to know."

"Oh yeah?"

"Me," the librarian says, and walks away, Izzy wordless, pinned to her seat.

Across from her, April's smiling, can't seem to stop.

"So what exactly do you need to get this done, businesswoman?" Izzy asks, dejected.

"I just got it," April says, and's

→ already walking into the biology lab in that here-from-the-office way, her pigtails making her invulnerable to suspicion.

All the begoggled students are cutting on pigs, some of their faces spattered with blood.

April goes sideways to slip around one of them, walks efficiently up to Mr. Victor, at his desk applying expiration-date labels to the pig baby jars ("*Never! It's formaldehyde!—Dr. V*").

"Yes, Ms. Ripley?" Mr. Victor says.

"So he didn't break them all, then?" April says, taking a jar in her hand.

"Give him time," Mr. Victor says, holding his hand across for whatever paper April's here to deliver, and April 'remembers,' has to shift hands to pass it across, thoughtlessly chock the jar she was inspecting up under her arm.

"April, April—" Mr. Victor says, standing, grabbing for the jar, but April's already spinning away like to see what he's worried about here: a spider? is her pen exploding in her chest pocket?

Just a jar full of pig baby, ma'am.

It shatters hard and April jumps away from the splash, knocking her wrist harder than necessary into a line of them, tipping another bottle over into open air.

Mr. Victor slips forward, just catches it by his fingertips, but the reach—a suspicious crunch involved with that, that he's already grimacing about—has left him stretched awkwardly across his tall desk, so that he can't see April stepping aside, extracting a number two pencil from behind her ear, using the eraser to nudge another jar off the *back* of the counter.

It explodes, splashing as high as the chalkboard.

"I'm so, so sorry, Mr. Victor," she says, her voice not at all matching with the face the rest of the class is seeing through their goggles.

She coughs once, into her hand, and, one by one the class gets it, a nod passing between them, and they start coughing, gagging.

"Vent hood, vent hood," Mr. Victor waves, and April reaches over, expertly turns it on with her pencil, blinking either innocently or in an evil way, it's hard to tell.

That fan starts sucking, moving what little hair Mr. Victor has left on his head.

"Did I mess up class?" April says earnestly, in a little-girl voice, "here, let me," and she takes the jar Mr. Victor managed to save, sets it up with the rest. "But I think it's on your—" she says, nodding to his crotch, somehow wet with formaldehyde. "Is that, is that bad for . . . *it?*"

Mr. Victor closes his eyes in mental pain,

→ passes Izzy and Brittany, getting a superlong drink from the fountain.

A moment after, April's swishing by.

"See you at the pep rally, *sister*," she says, and doesn't look back.

"I kind of hate her," Izzy says.

"Not the only one," Brittney says, pointing with her chin across the hall, to

→ what must be April's upper-level locker.

It got the same school photo/magnetic crown treatment.

Only, somebody's used a sharpie to drag an X across April's face.

"Wasn't me," Izzy says, stepping wide around it, her hands up by her shoulders like that's proof of her innocence, and

→ moments later they're stepping through shattered glass and baby pig, using forceps to open the big drawer of Mr. Victor's desk.

It's where he puts whatever he's confiscated.

Izzy digs, sorts, digs some more—tangled ear buds, a frisbee, cell phones, a plush wine bottle, something that might be sexual in nature, that Brittney won't touch when Izzy tries to pass it back—and finally comes up with the distinctive cell Mr. Victor took from Stuart the day before.

She punches a button and the screen lights up.

"Happy birthday to me," she says, sitting down behind the desk with Brittney, their two sets of boots Batman and Robin'd up on the wall.

"Happy birthday to *Crystal*," Brittney corrects.

"Nine, one . . . one," Izzy narrates, shutting her eyes to punch that last digit, sending us

→ winding down all the phone lines to a female mouth, a headset microphone bobbing before it.

"Please state the nature of your emergency," that dry voice says, and we hear a magazine page turning.

Back in the biology lab, Brittney holds the voice-changer across like a mike.

"*The sheriff was fun*," Izzy says. "*But over too fast. Don't worry, though . . . I'll be back.*"

She raises her shoulders to Brittney for an idea but Brittney's got nothing, so Izzy hangs up, turns around to put the phone back, and

→ in her POV, the janitor's standing there leaning on his mop, and, it's hard to tell with the hat, the coveralls, but . . . is that Ron Jeremy?

Surely not.

But maybe?

"Somebody reported a spill?" he says with that distinctive Queens lilt.

"We were just—we were just," Brittney says, clambering up with the desk's help, dropping Stuart's phone back into the prize drawer, shutting it unslyly with her knee.

Izzy stands behind her, trying to hide the voice changer.

"Scruffy?" Brittney says to the janitor, stabbing for a name.

Izzy elbows her.

"Not Norman," the janitor says, and salutes Izzy, turns around with his mop, whistling like he doesn't know what's going on in here, or who was here, or what they were doing.

On the way out the door, Izzy's already on her phone. Dialing the number off a card that has a Sheriff's star on it.

This time it rings and rings, Izzy and Brittney walking and walking, and finally a woman picks up.

"Um, yeah," Izzy says, "we just—I just heard you have somebody down there for something she's supposed to have done last night? Named Crystal? Well, you can't tell anybody, but, well. She was with me last night, okay? You can ask my parents, they were gone. She came over right after they left. We're . . . well. They don't approve, or wouldn't, so she had to wait. Nobody got pregnant's what I'm saying, if you follow? I kissed a girl and I liked it? But don't tell her dad, please. Oh, oh, I'm Isabelle Stratford, I'm sorry, Izzy I mean, I thought you knew, I don't know why, you don't have caller ID? But listen, I saw her earlier at the station but didn't know until now, I shouldn't be on the phone at school, Deputy Dante's already talked to me, he knows who I am, I've got to get to class, I just, just wanted to—"

Dial tone. Izzy's thumb the one that ended the call.

"Camping at Crystal Blake . . . " Brittney says. "Should I be jealous?"

"Ladies," Mr. Victor says, going the opposite way, his lab coat tucked around his waist, hiding his wet crotch.

"What happened?" Izzy says to him, fake concerned.

"Science can be a cruel mistress," he says, leaving Izzy and Brittney trying hard not to laugh.

"All right," Izzy says. "Save innocent girl who hates me, check. Almost be involved in a school shooting, check. Get kidnapped into homecoming, check."

"Get a date to the big dance, check and *mate*," Brittney says, swinging her hip over into Izzy, then sliding a condom package up like she always has it that handy: "Need anything for the big night?"

"You still use those ones?"

"Well, not the same one over and over . . . "

Izzy takes the condom and opens it, blows into it and ties it off so they can bat it back and forth as they walk, at least until Izzy says, "Hey, watch this," and sticks her tongue out, unscrews a ball off her tongue stud, presses the bottom of her tongue to the balloon.

It pops and they scream delight.

She keeps her chin up to twist the ball back onto the stud.

"We should really go to the pep-rally," Brittney says, taking Izzy's sleeve, redirecting them away from a harried Principal Masters jogging past, looking in all the classrooms, muttering to himself.

He stops as if to ask Izzy and Brittney something, sees that Izzy's still got a rubber in her hand then just "Never minds" them, like he knows better.

They watch him step into the biology lab, then:

"Pep-rally?" Izzy asks. "Why? Girls from *Cheerleader Camp* going to be there, or's it like that one Nirvana video?"

"Hope it's the Nirvana girls," Brittney says, "I'm fresh out of cigarettes," and then's rounding the corner with an unwilling Izzy. This time we don't go with them, are

→ swooping through the halls, heading for that front door, faster this time. Instead of exploding out into the sunlight like we keep wanting to, we stop at the trophy case then back up off it, looking up, up, through the mirror glare and shiny trophies of yesterday.

The sword.

It's gone.

Again.

We hear the *sound* of the pep-rally before it really focuses in— loud, screamy, chaos; very *Mo-ny, Mo-ny*—and then it's not the actual pep-rally itself but the gym hallway leading to it, a slurry of people making their way that way, Izzy and Brittney wading it, floating it, drowning in it.

"Remind me why we never come to these?" Izzy asks, getting jostled side to side.

Brittney doesn't answer, just pulls her ahead, to

→ a bubbling over Mrs. Graves, waiting at the doorway into the gym.

She holds her hand out sideways and Izzy looks in fear to Brittney, who's still got her by the arm.

"*No*," she says to Brittney.

"Do what scares you," Brittney says back, guiding her into Mrs. Graves, who's at the tail of a line of three girls:

April Ripley, smirking.

Mandy Kane, her thigh-highs striped red and white.

Lindsay Baker, the definition of regal.

"Take your place among high school royalty, check," Brittney says, smiling for Izzy.

Before Izzy can find a way out, she's been pushed into line and they're

→ making their way out onto the gym floor, the crowd chanting Ti-*tans!* Ti-*tans!*

Lindsay parade-waves with her good arm, and Mandy tries to match that.

April just looks out across the crowd coolly.

Izzy's glaring straight ahead, like this is a death march.

Once they get to what can only be called a dais, Lindsay looking down to not catch a heel on the step, we

→ swing around behind them, get the full effect of this many screaming students.

The stands are packed, the gym decked out.

Up front, Izzy's POV singles out Brittney, smiling for her. Izzy directs her eyes purposefully away, sees, off to the side, trying to get a good angle on all these people, Jamie. Taking picture after picture.

"But you don't have access," Izzy recites,

→ tilting her head Jamie-ward for Brittney and Brittney already knows, steams her eyes up about it.

"*Go, Titans!*" a woman up front screams into the microphone then, redirecting everybody's energy to the front, letting them know this thing's about to start.

The noise dies down.

Jamie's camera POV swings around to the microphone, gets that woman in his crosshairs, and it's . . . Izzy's mom?

His *click* cuts us to

→ Izzy, stepping back far enough that April has to reach back, catch her from splatting off the dais.

"Mommy dearest, right?" April says, using her other hand to let her hair down, swish it all around dramatically, transforming her.

"More like Pamela Voorhees," Izzy says, and Lindsay turns her glittering smile over to Izzy, interrogating them with her smile.

"Mrs. Voorhees loved her son," Lindsay says primly, in a please-shut-up-now way, and Izzy's so shocked that she lets April reel her back into this homecoming line-up.

"As elected queen of . . . well, let's just say a few years ago, shall we?" Izzy's mom leads off, "it's my pleasure to present to you this year's homecoming court!"

She turns to lead the clapping and everybody claps enough, anyway.

"I thought pep-rallies were about football," Izzy says, and Mandy accidentally grins.

"Are we supposed to give speeches?" Izzy hisses then, but Lindsay's already stepping up to the microphone, Principal Masters rising to adjust it for her in a way that—angling that mike to her mouth—looks especially lecherous. It doesn't help that he's having to reach around her sides to do it.

Lindsay wows her eyes out at the awkwardness of this and takes the mike in her own hand, her good hand, and says, trying to take the attention away from Masters, already retreating to the wings, "It's been a tough couple of weeks for us, I won't lie. We've lost some heroes. But we can't let that stop us, can we? No, we can't. If they were here, they'd be on the field tomorrow night, or up here alongside me. But they're not. So that leaves the burden on all of us to step up, doesn't it? Now, as you can see, the homecoming court, since it was so last-minute, and since I was the last remaining member, I was given the honor of selecting it, isn't that wonderful? And—and the past weekend taught me a lot. It taught me that a good horse will always go back to the barn at the end of the day, no matter how far away that barn is. It taught me, it taught me who to *value*. It taught me that life isn't a beauty pageant, or a popularity contest, that the least likely can be the most important, that friendship can come from the most unexpected places. Now, let's hear it for your Danforth homecoming court!"

Less excited applause.

"Take it off!" somebody yells—a girl.

"Where's Crystal!" a lone guy yells, probably Davis, and other guys agree, and a couple of the male teachers.

Lindsay leans forward for the microphone. "One of us is absent, yes, but she's here in spirit, and sends her sincerest regrets, I'm sure. But you can still vote for her. The boxes are at the main office, and are due by school's end tomorrow, okay? And please just vote once, no matter how much you love and believe in these girls!"

Scattered laughter for that, anyway, and then the lights dim and we go tighter on Lindsay, a lone trumpet cueing up off-camera, ethereal and mournful

→ (Izzy's underbreath response: "*Seriously?*" Her eyes incredulous that nobody's calling foul on this);

→ Mrs. Graves grinning proudly, her tissue balled in her hand, her hand over her chest;

→ Jamie kneeing his way up to the edge of Lindsay's disc of *Tron* light, to get her ascension from a low angle;

→ Mandy reaching the side of her hand for April's, for sisterhood, for joy, April *not* letting that happen;

→ Izzy's mom angling her head over, her POV looking away from a line of six guys lifting their shirts in unison, to show their chests;

→ Brittney holding up a fastmade sign—notebook paper, black marker—for Izzy: "*my unicorn girl!*" and blinking away tears above it, or acting like it, anyway;

→ Izzy slyly flipping her off in return, except now she's turning her head, counting heads, whispering names: "*Mandy, Ripley, Blake*—oh shit."

"As many of you read in today's paper," Lindsay starts off, blinking the emotions away, it looks like, giving us a flash to zoom in on

→ Izzy's mouth, no voice, just the shape, the realization: *They're all final girls.*

Brittney's response is a truly lost "What?" but we heard Izzy loud and clear, are doing that mental math, trying to connect names.

She's right.

"Last weekend was a harrowing ordeal," Lindsay goes on, her voice almost cracking. "But what I learned from that experience is that every day, any day, can be a harrowing ordeal. But a worthwhile one, right? Tests, applications, jobs, relationships, doctors' offices—sorry, Daddy—practices . . . *football* games . . . "

With her emphasis the jerseyed football players in the front row stand and she leads the applause for them, and, while they're standing, the Titan mascot comes barreling out from a side door, stumbling as if pushed.

And he's got the sword, is leading a pretend charge with it.

The crowd erupts,

→ Jamie wheeling to photodocument this, the lights still down so Titan gets kind of a strobe effect from his flash, and, those freeze frames . . . something's not quite right, here.

"They're all final girls," Izzy says again to Brittney, and this time Brittney gets it, looks down the line, finally swinging her POV back to Izzy, that POV switching to Izzy's now, for Brittney's question, fastwritten on the back of her piece of notebook paper: "What about U?"

"What about *Lindsay*," Izzy says to herself, looking over just as Lindsay invites Titan up onto the stage, latches onto his thick neck with her good arm, pulling him into her spotlight, reaching back for a . . . long black tube?

The crowd stands, stomping—this is a ritual they know, evidently. But first:

→ the spotlight splits in two, tracks across the floor to the same side door that birthed Titan, holds there.

"And of course, what's a Queen without a King, right?" Lindsay says.

→ ("A woman?" Izzy asks, squinting even to hear Lindsay saying this.)

And then Lindsay makes a show of turning to her court.

"And, I'm kind of springing this on all of you, now, girls, I hope you don't mind. Some of you didn't even know you were going to be front and center for this, I know, so it would be too much for me to ask you to *also* bring a date."

"*What?*" Izzy says, with her whole face.

April's got a better response: "That bitch."

"Jerry, Jerry!" Mandy says, waving a football player up to stand alongside her.

"Well, we know how to make do, don't we?" Lindsay says, hitching the microphone under her arm to lead yet another round of applause.

"Was that a compliment?" Jerry says to Mandy and April and Izzy.

"This is all for her," Izzy says, and she's right: Lindsay's already turned back around, commandeering the crowd's attention.

"But for me, as you all of course know"—that lone trumpet shifting down to melancholy, now—"my King can't, he can't be with us this weekend. Or ever again. Except in our hearts." She touches her own to show, somehow managing to bring her halogen-white sling even more in the spotlight. "But this is homecoming, right? *Right?*"

Mrs. Graves leads this round of perfunctory applause.

"Wait," Izzy, clapping, says to April, pointing to the mascot. "You're him, aren't you? Titan?"

"Past tense," April says, clapping as well. "I guess Masters found a replacement."

Izzy studies this Titan, but this show's still the All-Lindsay Power Hour:

"Now, there was some excitement at school this morning—another test—but real tragedy avoids the pure of heart, as I've learned, but what many of us failed to acknowledge this morning was the true hero of the hour," the lights dipping down to even darker, "*my* date for tomorrow night, my running mate on the ballot, as it were—vote Lindsay and Jake!"

Absolutely silent on Izzy's face, even though the whole gym's screaming.

The betrayal, the shock, her head shaking no. Her POV watching mummy-faced Jake walk out like he didn't deserve that intro, that he was just doing his job, the applause swelling louder and louder, everybody standing to do it.

He hops up onto the stage, slips an arm around Lindsay's waist.

"Hey, hey, really," he says, "I was just fucking around, right? Oops," Mrs. Graves trying to blink this profanity away, clapping louder as if she can erase it with school spirit.

Jake manages to wave all the clapping down, then steps away—we can tell this is all scripted; the revulsion is Izzy's and ours both—presents Lindsay, who raises her shoulders as if this is a departure.

"*Real* heroes, they don't fuck around," he says, and, reaches behind her for a rope that should just be for gym class, for climbing.

But it's been repurposed.

Now what it does is dislodge something big and bulky up in the rafters.

Instead of getting to see it at first, we watch the crowd's reaction.

It's mostly screaming. Some of it real, actual scared screaming. Then back to

→ whatever's . . . . not falling, but un*furl*ing.

The spotlight finally settles on it.

A banner, the words on it THE NIGHT HE CAME HOME in a spooky font, except "HE" is crossed out, "*Bulldogs*" in its place.

"Beat the Bulldogs!" Lindsay screams into the microphone, and then Jake pulls on the rope harder.

This time an obvious body tumbles down through the spotlight, jerks to a hung stop about five feet off the gym floor, jouncing on its rope, its neck somehow holding.

The spotlight tracks down the rope, tracks down, and . . .

It's Billie Jean.

But different.

He's clothes stuffed with rags, a dummy, the mask tied to a broom-as-backbone.

"Billie Jean" swings back and forth, close enough to Lindsay and Titan that they have to duck sideways.

That lone trumpet's gone, replaced by a line of trombones like a heartbeat, speeding up, the tuba punctuating it, jacking our nerves up higher, so that it's almost a comfort to look over to

→ the source of all this: the shape of the band teacher, his forehead sweaty, brass glinting in the darkness all around.

"But the good side always wins, right, Lindsay?" Jake goes on, his lines memorized, and Lindsay makes a show of remembering that long black tube she's holding. That this is a pep-rally, not real life.

She thrusts the tube out at Titan, holding the open end to him, and he looks to the crowd again, waiting, waiting, and, because they've done this before, their stomping swells and swells—Mandy and Jerry having to lean over to duck "Billie Jean" now—and, finally, the moment they've all been waiting for: Titan steps up to Lindsay, leading with the sword, to push it into the tube she's wedged under her sling for him, but she has to guide the sword with her good hand

→ ("everything's phallic," Izzy narrates)

→ Lindsay raising her hand to her mouth to lick a small line of blood that we file in our heads, for later, just because that's what we do, and then, like this isn't already sexual enough, Titan thrusts the sword into that sheath, and thrusts it again even deeper, the crowd absolutely going wild now.

When he pulls it out it's dripping with liquid.

"Is nothing sacred?" Izzy says to April.

"That doesn't smell right," April says back, her clapping slowing, her POV flashing out for the wall of the gym, it looks like.

For what?

"But who, who," Lindsay says, leaning forward to peer into the darkness, talking with the kind of voice you'd talk to Lassie with, telling us this is part of the ritual, "we need a flame, don't we? Does anybody out there have one? Not at school, surely? Whatever shall we do?"

Laughter. Groans.

"But maybe the teachers will look away just for a minute, do you think?" Lindsay says. "Teachers, please, can you look away for a moment? We'll be good, we promise?"

Jamie pivots around to the crowd, his camera POV clicking on

→ Mr. Pleasance, politely clapping his completely bored agreement;

→ Mr. Victor, still wearing his lab coat like a skirt, raising his clapping hands to make a show his super-sincere school spirit, and, finally;

→ Mrs. Graves, raising her fist like *Yes!*

The crowd swells with stomping, faster and faster, thunderous. This is really going to happen, the

→ drum line coming on hard and loud now, stepping out onto the floor,

→ one of the shirtless dudes crowd surfing.

At the height of it all Lindsay leans down to the microphone.

"But . . . none of you have a flame of pure school spirit, do you?"

We wheel around behind her, a disorienting ride but it shows what's in front of her, like magic: out in the stands, lighters come on everywhere.

"Oh, good, good," she says. "There's so much spirit in the air today!" Lindsay says in her little girl voice. "Now, if one of you could just—"

"Can we please get this over with already," Izzy interrupts, stepping forward with her zippo.

Lindsay slashes her eyes to Izzy but doesn't lose her winning smile.

"It's only fitting," Lindsay says, and directs Titan's sword to Izzy.

Izzy lights her lighter, Titan holds the sword over it, and it flares up, big enough that April slashes her hands out to Izzy and Mandy, pushing them back, keeping them away from this heat.

"No, it's gas!" she says to Titan, but her voice is lost in the craziness.

And this sword, it does look pretty excellent in the darkness.

Out of nowhere then, "Billie Jean" taps into Izzy from behind.

She flinches away, embarrassed, and pushes him forward, past her.

He comes right back, so she has to step aside,

"Who are we playing?" she says to herself, "the John Carpenters?"

Billie Jean goes spinning past, into Titan.

He takes advantage, stabs his sword clean through it.

→ the no-joke point slicing right between Mandy and Jerry

→ the flame all scraped off, onto Billie Jean, who's reacting just as the sword did to the flame, meaning *he* was soaked too, but

→ "No," Mrs. Graves says, her clapping braking to a worried halt, "I told them they couldn't do that part." Still:

→ Billie Jean flares up, and, because he was just filled with rags, Titan's sword has gone deep enough that the arm of his costume is deep in the chest, meaning

→ that sleeve's lit as well, now.

"*Fire extinguisher!*" April yells to the audience as Titan goes rolling out onto the gym floor, trying to douse these flames, but they're fast. He's a fireball.

It's terrible.

He's right at the feet of all the football players, too, who finally start taking their shirts off, trying to blanket Titan.

Their jerseys are just as flammable.

Finally a gout of dry whiteness clouds down onto Titan, and we track back up that stream to

→ Mrs. Graves, using this fire extinguisher like Jesse Ventura, and screaming behind it.

The students around her step away.

Titan's out, is just smoking.

"Is it Masters?" Izzy says, stepping in, fighting through, looking around.

"The head, the head!" April's screaming now. "He can't breathe!"

She goes to pull it off but has to fall back, the fabric still smoldering, her hands gummy with melted mascot fur.

"Here," an offscreen Jake says behind her, nudging her aside with the sword.

He angles it into the neck, rips the head away, and inside it's a mess, is the harshest gore since the opening scene.

Skin baked down to bone, melted off, hair scorched, one eyeball wheeling around in terror.

"*Dead and Buried*," Izzy says to herself.

"More like Cropsy," Brittney says, right there beside her, and Izzy looks up to her, sees how shaken Brittney is.

She takes her hand.

"It was my flame," Izzy says to Brittney.

"You knew," Brittney says, "how?" and Jamie settles his crosshairs on the two of them there like that and snaps his shutter on the sad scene, delivering us to

→ the Sheriff's offices, Dante ushering a not-handcuffed Crystal Blake past a desk.

"Dante?" the woman deputy says, standing from a desk, a beige phone still in her hand.

Before she can say anything, a fire truck's sirens whip past.

"Another?" he says to the deputy.

The deputy's eyes tell the story.

The school parking lot again. For the second time this day. It's snarled with emergency vehicles, with media vans, with concerned parents.

The sound of a helicopter blade whipping, whipping.

A smoking gurney is being wheeled out to that helicopter, the police holding their hats to their heads, guiding these paramedics to the helicopter's waiting door just as Alice Cooper comes on loud, telling us that school's out for summer, even though the leaves are red and gold.

We drift

→ inside with this music, to Principal Masters in his office, tranced out, bouncing a racquetball against the wall again and again;

→ Mrs. Graves walking the halls, looking in each doorway;

→ a fireman, smelling this long black tube;

→ Lindsay, dragging this heavy sword one-handed, the tip scraping along the floor;

→ Billie Jean, smoldering on his rope, motionless now;

→ mummy-faced Jake in the biology lab, having a Yorrick moment with a jar of pig baby;

→ what must be Mandy's school photo on her locker.
It's X'd out, now.
She walks up to it oblivious, opens it

→ delivering us to Izzy and Brittney and her mom, standing from the car in Izzy's garage, Izzy still hauling that knee brace.

"Well, in my day they just used rubbing alcohol or something," Izzy's mom is saying.

Izzy slams her door shut.

Brittney's still shell-shocked, her eyes red from crying.

"Maybe it was supposed to be more dramatic," Izzy says. "The only pep rally visible from space."

"There was always a homecoming bonfire, I guess," her mother says, pushing in to

→ the house.

"And you still don't have a date?" her mom continues, to Izzy.

"*Still?*" Izzy says.

"'Anymore,' whatever," her mom says. "You're young, you'll heal. It's part of it."

"*Theresa*," Brittney says then, looking up to Izzy, with wonder.

Izzy narrows her eyes at Brittney but doesn't pursue.

"And you never told me you were homecoming queen," Izzy says to her mom. "I knew you grew up here, but that seems like, I don't know. Vital information to pass along?"

"I didn't want to pressure you to succeed."

"Or highlight my many failings?"

"About your escort," her mom says. "Would you say there are prospects?"

"The sheriff's dead, Mom, and the janitor's dying, and we just buried six kids last week. Do you really think my having a date for a stupid dance is really the key issue?"

"Or is somebody trying to deflect?" her mom says.

"I'm not going to win, Mom. We're just there to make Lindsay look better. She practically said so."

"You're a winner just for being in her court."

"*Her* court. Thanks for the support. You know she's just stacking Jake in because he got hurt, right? Nobody can see his face, so everybody'll have to be looking at her. It'll be dramatic for the yearbook. They're the perfect pair. The supermodel and the invisible man."

"In spite of all this social acumen, though—Brittney, will she have an escort?"

"Ummm," Brittney says.

"I *can* go alone, Mom," Izzy says. "There's no shame in—"

"Your father will take you. One of the girls in my court, her boyfriend had to ship out unexpectedly for the war, so her father stepped in. It was very nice, very proper, almost like a wedding. The crowd loved it. She probably should have won. I probably should have given the crown to her, except. Well. I only had the one, right?"

"Mom. I'm not letting Dad anywhere near—"

"I'll make him . . . dress up," Izzy's mom says, and of course we know she's saying she'll keep him sober. "He'll be so proud. His two homecoming girls. A family tradition."

"Well this should really be a night to remember," Izzy says, jerking the refrigerator door open, blocking her mom from her view, from her life.

"Theresa is long for *Terry*," Brittney says, now. "And Terry is a boy's name too."

"And—okay," Izzy says. "Final girls have names that go both ways, AC/DC, and maybe that's a social shield or something, keeps them virgins longer than the rest of us. Ripley, Blake, Mandy. I'm with you."

"Lindsay *Theresa* Baker," Brittney says. "I remember it from third grade. Jake used to call her 'Lieutenant,' for her initials."

"So that just leaves me then, right?" Izzy says, taking a whole container of leftover something under her arm. "'Izzy,' buy me at Starbucks. Deflowered apple of her father's eye. Cusses like a sailor who went to cussing school, smokes like a ballerina, drinks like a Nascar fan, studies like a . . . like *you*. Can you remember anybody like me on any final girl roster?"

Brittney shakes her head no.

"Then what am I doing up there?" Izzy says, shutting the refrigerator, walking away but we stay there, on the dry-erase board, her family's running grocery list, evidently.

Underlined with an angry slash: *burritos?*

"I'm just saying," Brittney's saying, her and Izzy walking down the hill toward the river, Brittney carrying the leftovers now, Izzy the knee brace. "I don't think it's a slasher yet. One dead cop, one disfigured janitor. Those don't a slasher make. I don't even think either of them were having sex when they got it. Isn't it supposed to be about all your *friends* dying, right? Until only you're left, have to face your own personal demon?"

"Careful what you wish for," Izzy says, fighting a branch. "My friend is you."

Brittney slows, realizing this.

"It's Lindsay," Izzy says, seeing the sheriff's badge in the leaf litter. She steps on it, holds a branch aside for Brittney to pass. "Fucking karma," she says to herself, about the badge, looking from it to Brittney, walking ahead, so alive. So not dead.

"Karma?" Brittney calls back.

"It's Lindsay," Izzy repeats, falling in. "Well, first, she's the definition of batshit. And I say that as a certified crazy person. It takes one to know one. But second, I think she's scared."

"Of losing the crown?"

"She's always had the crown, and, with school cancelled tomorrow, how many votes do you think are going to trickle in? No, what she's scared of is that they never found the body."

"Billie Jean."

"She doesn't think it's over yet. She knows the genre better than she lets on, has to hide it because only losers get their thrills in the horror section, right? But she's seen *Maniac*, *New York Ripper*, all the down and dirty stuff, all the video nasties. And she learned from it, like I did. She knows she's still the perfect target, the source of imaginary revenge, the end result of some escaped lunatic's twisted logic—"

"Her dad's."

"Yeah. But what she's doing—she's insulating herself the best way she knows. If it is all about the people around you dying, then she's specifically chosen a group to be around that she doesn't care about, right? That she probably thinks the yearbook would be better without. Crystal, who's prettier than her. April, who's smarter. Mandy, who's trying to be her clone. And—"

"And you."

"And me, her exact opposite. We're all story padding. Bodies Billie Jean's going to have to carve through to get to her. I should write a paper on it for Pleasance."

Brittney stops, looks back.

"And you're not worried?"

"That little dumb show at the pep rally? She was overcompensating. Trying to tell the whole school she's not afraid, that she faced Billie Jean down and lived to make jokes about it."

"Either that or calling him out," Brittney says, almost stepping into the suddenly-there creek.

Izzy pulls her back, barely.

"Calling *me* out, more like," Izzy says, and Brittney looks up to her.

"Jake?"

"She can have any guy she wants, and she chose him."

"But she's—if you're right, she's setting it up so she's the final girl of all the final girls, isn't she? The *queen* of the final girls."

"If it even goes that far," Izzy says, squatting down by her tree, ferreting a yellow ski rope up from the leaf litter. "But you're right. This isn't a slasher. Not yet."

"Then what is it?"

Izzy looks across the water wistfully.

"You know that moment in the high school romantic comedy where the bookworm reject charity case lets her hair down, takes her glasses off and walks down the stairs a stone cold fox on top of the world?"

Brittney's POV looks over at Izzy, shaking her hair around, pulling her Buddy Hollies off, the dying sun right behind her.

"This is that," Izzy says, and whips the yellow cord back,

→ our POV dizzying up above them, looking down on the two of them standing there, a blanket of leaf-litter hunting camo whipping away from the prone form of Billie Jean, staked to the ground with camping equipment.

Brittney steps back, screams to make Janet Leigh roll over in her grave, the leftovers falling from her hands.

Izzy grins, watching Billie Jean's bloodshot eyes, seeming to drink this sound in.

"He liked that," she says. "Shit. And here I've just been feeding him burritos."

Brittney takes another step back, looks up to the house. Comes back to Izzy. "That's—that's why you needed the brace," she finally manages to get out, about to either laugh or scream again, it's hard to tell.

"Lindsay's right," Izzy says, collecting the leftovers. "Billie Jean *is* coming back for her. With a little help from his friends."

"So . . . so is this a horror movie now, or a teen comedy?" Brittney says.

"It's an afterschool special," Izzy says, Hoddering her head over to study Billie Jean. "Know what the take-home message is? Don't fuck with Izzy Stratford."

"Can't 'Izzy' be a boy's name too?"

"Shut up. I'm having a moment here."

"You are batshit," Brittney says, impressed.

"Got to be, these days," Izzy says, and drops to one knee, cracks open the leftovers, Billie Jean lunging for them in his broken way.

"He's cute," Brittney says, coming in beside Izzy.

"Just don't get too close," Izzy says, and holds a spoonful across the void,

→ our POV lining up with Billie Jean's slashercam angle: through two Michael-ish eyeholes, these two teen girls are right there, so close.

His breathing accelerates, matches up with

→ Jamie's. He's still working his camera at school, just not the gym anymore, but the trophy case, Principal Masters and Mrs. Graves and Deputy Dante all there at the edge of this photo opportunity, the rest of the hall deserted.

One-armed Lindsay is putting the sword back where it belongs.

Flash, *flash*, and, in the last pic she looks back, smiles this absolutely killer smile and we cut to

→ thick chains passing through two institutional door handles, then clanking tight, and somehow tighter.

Backing up, it's the front doors to the school.

And it's Dante applying the padlock, testing the doors, flexing his biceps.

They're tight. His arms *and* the chains.

He holds the key up for Masters and Graves to see, then delicately places it on his tongue, swallows it.

"But—but the dance, it's tomorrow night," Mrs. Graves says, looking around for support.

"Call me about four o'clock," Dante says. "Men's bathroom at the Texaco. This shit ends tonight."

"Sh-sh—?" Mrs. Graves says, sure she's hearing wrong. "Tonight? But what about the Texaco?"

"Figure of speech," Dante says. "No more deaths on my watch. There's a new sheriff in town, people. One who doesn't take any— it's the end of the killings, I mean. Right here, right now. No more

accidents, no more bodies. This is my town."
Principal Masters

→ directs his POV away from all this stupidity, to the helicopter banking away on the other side of town.
So serene, so idyllic.
We know where we are, though.
This is the calm before the massacre.

NO
INTERMII'S'SION

Across town, somewhere *under* that helicopter, down deeper in the trees than Dante can see is the creek again, always.

We're right down at the surface of it, looking across it, lingering long enough that it's starting to feel like filler, like stock footage, 'sunset in a small town,' except . . . is that trash and flotsam on the far bank about to resolve into a Halloween mask?

Is another body going to come floating past?

Is Billie Jean going to step down into the water, his blank eyes neither grim nor hungry?

Is that water that's slightly out of focus in the foreground about to go red?

On the bank at the back of the frame, a turtle—the same one we saw earlier?—slips soundlessly into the water, and, just when we're watching that part of the bank, thinking maybe that smart turtle slipped into the creek *ahead* of whatever's coming, something shrikes down through the surface of the water fast and hard right in front of us, close enough that it's just a dark shape, a violent cleaving, but

→ backing off a bit, it's the thick blade of a long black sword.

The water steams away from it like it knows this thing is pure evil, and the creek churns and eddies around it, trying to heal this wound.

But the injury's been done.

"*Take it! Take it!*" a kid's voice screams, and we

→ swirl out, up to the bridge where the sixth graders are, and something about our angle, about our limited view—it feels like an unclaimed POV. Like somebody's watching.

Down in the water Ben's slinging his hand around, the oven mitt it's in smoking, leaf boy and the hesitant kid standing back, out of the way, no longer as committed to this as they probably were moments ago.

"Shit shit *shit!*" Ben's saying, throwing the mitt away, sucking on his fingers.

The sword's just standing there in the current, and we can't look away. Not because it's pure and deadly and impossible and unlikely, but because . . . do we recognize it?

It's pretty much just a long slab of hammered metal with a folded-on-itself rebar hilt. Like something you'd cut out of cardboard, just, this time, the cardboard was metal.

It's that sword we glimpsed earlier, the one being forged in a cellar.

It was *Ben* making it.

"Isn't this kind of like asking for it?" the hesitant kid says, studying the sword.

"From Billie Jean or from his mom?" leaf boy says, circling the sword appreciatively, collecting the oven mitt from the water.

"She's spaced on Xanax half the time she's in the basement anyway," Ben says. "Like she's going to notice one missing piece of metal?"

"It's not even sharp," the hesitant kid says, splashing water up onto the sword.

The handle hisses steam.

"That's what the grinder's for, dill hole," Ben says, and reaches over for the handheld grinder, its battery snugged into the handle, blinking green and ready.

He hits the trigger, spinning that grinding wheel, and it's so loud

→ and so close

→ that we look ahead, to the end of that awkward sharpening job: Ben's in a dramatic shower of sparks in the middle of the creek, the other two using the mitt and a t-shirt to hold the blade in place, both edges shiny and dangerous now, Ben just finishing the point with flourish, ramping that grinding wheel up into the air, letting the sound die.

"More like it," Ben says, tossing the grinder up onto the bank, commandeering the sword, lightsabering it into the hesitant kid's neck lightly, in slow motion, doing the sound effects himself, saying just for himself, "Will you come back more powerful than I could possibly imagine?"

But the blade's still hot from the grinding.

The hesitant kid flinches back, goes under the water, comes up with a bloody neck and betrayed eyes.

"Guess not," Ben says.

"Shit," leaf boy says, looking to Ben.

"It's tasted human blood now," Ben says, holding the sword flat to study it, to be in proper awe of it, and then a tall shadow ripples out across the surface of the water they're standing in.

Slowly, they all look up to it.

"Oh," Ben says, and we hear a car slurping by

→ and, inside *a* car, anyway—now, later, we don't know—Izzy's driving, Brittney in the passenger seat, which Brittney's still in awe of.

"Can't believe she let you take it," Brittney's saying, touching the leather with her palms, luxuriating in it.

"I'm her real daughter now," Izzy says, dimming and brightening the headlights like a game, to show us it's full dark. "Homecoming beauty, part two. The next generation."

Both of them have their seat belts on. No cigarettes. Boots on the floor mats.

"What if it *was* your mom?" Brittney says, watching the trees glide by. "Billie Jean, I mean."

"My mom who we left in the house before walking down to see him, or some secret mom I don't know about?"

"I know, I know, but—she's the surprise queen from yesterday, right? And now this new crop of girls is trying to replace her, make everybody forget her? What could be more perfect?"

"*Sea of Love,*" Izzy says, clocking her rearview. "It's my dad doing it all, since my brother's, you know."

"Too obvious," Brittney says. "It has to be the secretly-evil last person you'd ever expect, right? Not the obvious evil person."

"You?"

"Am I that obvious?"

"But maybe the expected's gone full circle," Izzy says, staring straight ahead. "Maybe it's so obvious now that that's the only thing that *can* be a surprise."

"I think you're not looking under the mask because you're scared."

Izzy looks over to Brittney about this.

"That it's going to be somebody you know," Brittney fills in, "instead of somebody Lindsay knows."

"They found my brother," Izzy says. "Nice family out waterskiing the next day. Very *Sleepaway Camp*. Closed casket. Nice way to gloom it up, though."

"I wasn't—"

"You can't look under the mask," Izzy goes on. "If you look under the mask, that means the fun's over. It's not bullets or fire or telekinesis or lightning or sequels or the economy that kills a slasher, it's being unmasked. Seen Kiss anywhere lately? Anyway, it's her show, Lindsay. So it's her dad."

"He's an orthopedist, right?" Brittney says, pulling her burring phone up. "Don't they fix knees and stuff?"

"Physician, heal thyself," Izzy answers, and, kind of to herself, grinning: "With burritos."

"Hey," Brittney says, reading her phone. "You were right. There's a party tonight. Bogey's."

"You don't have to be aware of the formula to fall victim to it," Izzy shrugs, pulling up in front of the video store, her headlights glaring off the front glass. "Everybody's a walking cliché."

"Except you, with your hair and your piercings and your attitude, that retro Q you got going on."

"Ever point that high-powered perception at yourself, Clarice?"

"Just promise you won't untie him without calling me first."

"So you can watch?"

"So I can go to church," Brittney smiles, commandeering the mirror to sloppy-bun her hair up, do her lips. "Maybe invent a revirgining machine."

"Hymenator 2000," Izzy says, liking it. "'Guaranteed to make you invulnerable to slashers, endorsed by four out of five final girls.' Let me know when you get it going?"

They bump fists stupidly.

"Sucks that Jake fell through," Brittney says. "I know—you haven't gotten any since moving here, right?"

"Affairs of the heart or affairs of the backseat?"

"Both. Either. All of the above. Unless you were, you know,

serious about you and Crystal McCrazy Chick."

"Boys at this school don't know what they're missing," Izzy says.

Brittney reaches across and they hug, and,

→ close on Izzy's face, she's actually satisfied here.

We go around behind her, though, for Brittney's face, and it's completely different. She's not paying attention to this hug anymore at all.

"You might not be the only one in a movie," she says, pushing away, directing Izzy's eyes through the windshield, and

→ their over-the-leather-dash POV has Jamie deep in the video shelves, trying to find just the right one.

"You know he's the stranger in town," Izzy says, caution in her tone.

"The good-looking stranger in town," Brittney says, slithering her bra out her left sleeve, tossing it up on the dash. "Everybody's got their Jake, right? Isn't that some rule of the world?"

"You've got protection anyway, right?"

Brittney cracks her purse.

Inset, it's *all* condoms.

Britt, mostly offscreen: "Thirty-one flavors."

"Was thinking more along the lines of," Izzy says, opening the console, digging, digging.

"Your dad's pills?" Brittney says, opening her door, the dome light glowing on. "Haven't you heard? I put the V in Viagra. I'm the non-pharmaceutical solution. I come to the pool, *none* of the boys get out of the water."

All Izzy finds is the rhinestone studded *case* for the stun gun, though. She holds it, remembering that arc of spark. Mad at herself.

"Just be careful tonight," Izzy says, shutting the console. "What time do you get off?"

"Depends on Johnny Depp in there," Brittney says.

"If he's not really Krug," Izzy says. "We should really have a curfew, think? We're way too horny and stupid to stay alive without supervision."

"Speaking of," Brittney says, checking her face in the visor mirror now, popping her lips like she does, "Going to the big party without me?"

"Got to dig up a dress for tomorrow night," Izzy says, hopelessly. "One that goes with these," her combat boots.

"I've got twenty," Brittney says. "My dad thinks I'm a princess, and my mom babysits me with her MasterCard."

"So we're really splitting up here," Izzy says.

"It's not that kind of movie," Brittney says, standing, undoing one more button on her blouse, arranging her chest like a Venus eyetrap. "Remember?"

And then she's gone.

"Said the nubile co-ed," Izzy tags on, and drops the car into REVERSE

→ just to screech to an instant stop when somebody slams their hands down onto her trunk.

Big in her rearview, it's Billie Jean.

"I'm walking here!" he quotes.

Some football player in a Billie Jean mask, anyway.

"Everybody wants to live forever," Izzy says, and taps the gas pedal, chirping the tires, stabbing back at this football player, her bumper touching the knees of his jeans,

→ but, back in her rearview mirrored POV, a truly huge form takes shapes *behind* this Billie Jean.

Izzy turns fast in her seat, and her through-the-back-window POV shows it's not the real Billie Jean yet, but Dante.

He lifts the football player *by* the mask until the mask slurps off, taking hair with it, and a fair amount of dignity.

Outside the car, now, with them and this scene, Dante extends his hand out, uses his Morpheus fingers to invite the rest of the football players into his vicinity.

They slouch in, groaning.

"Shouldn't you be sleeping?" Dante says to them all, his toothpick red now. "Watching tapes, humping your pillow? Big game tomorrow, right? Might be the last time in your lives you get to save the day. Walk into the dance at eleven like goddamn heroes. You've got the rest of your lives to be this stupid, and I trust that you're going to take full advantage no matter what I say. Right now, though, this school needs something to believe in. You can give that to them tomorrow night."

Lowered heads, a mumbled round of *yessirs*.

Dante looks from face to face, nods, then cocks his pepper spray up, fills the mask with it.

"Save it for tomorrow night, gentlemen," Dante says, "and if I hear of anymore of *this* bullshit"—throwing the mask into the chest of this former Billie Jean—"then . . . let's just say Billie Jean won't be your own personal boogeyman anymore, yeah?"

The boys shuffle away grumbling, the mask left behind.

Izzy's still twisted around to see through the back window so's startled by the single knock on her window.

It's Dante, of course.

"Thanks," she says, hating to have to say it.

"Just doing my job," Dante says, tipping his stiff hat. "Here for a rental?"

"No school tomorrow, day of mourning, all that."

"Stay up however late then, right?"

"You're doing it wrong, you know," Izzy says, both hands on the wheel, brakes still flared.

"What?" Dante says. "Keeping you all from killing yourselves?"

Izzy nods yes, that.

"You're not supposed to believe us until it's too late. You're for cleanup, not prevention."

Dante laughs his bassoon laugh.

"Don't tell anybody I told you this, Stratford," he says. "But you're all right, you know? You keep it interesting."

"Glad to be of service," Izzy says, only partially in this conversation anymore, her POV tracking Brittney, working her way down a shelf to Jamie, who is still unaware of her.

Or, waiting like a spider.

"Well, you better get this wreck home, then," Dante says, patting the shiny roof, standing away from the side mirror.

Izzy looks up to him, her eyes hot, and backs up about three feet.

And stops, like she's made a decision.

"So who switched the gasoline in at the pep-rally?" she says through the window.

Dante just stares at her.

"You know I can't speak about pending bullshit," he says. "Especially bullshit just about anybody in that goddamn school could have done. For any of a thousand piss-ant reasons, not the least of which is plain stupidity."

Izzy smiles. Somebody's finally being honest with her.

"The gasoline," she says, in trade, "it wasn't for Carl."

"The janitor?"

"April was supposed to be the one to die."

To show what she means, she traces an X over her own face. Just like the one on April's locker.

"She was up on stage, though," Izzy goes on. "Easy to forget, she's been Titan for so long. Or maybe she was supposed to be this time, even, but decided not to at the last moment."

"And how would you know all this?" Dante says, stepping closer again.

"Did my homework," Izzy says, throwing her eyes over the hood, to the bright, blinking video store. "And it's not over yet either," she adds, unwrapping a piece of her mother's nicotine gum now, depositing it into her mouth, squinting from that rancid taste.

Dante just stares at her.

"Who?" he finally says.

"Billie Jean would be my guess," Izzy says, looking both ways, "or somebody who looks just like him," and, when the coast is clear, she scribbles something on the inside of the gum wrapper. "You on all night?" she says to Dante.

"Until this is over or I am," Dante growls.

"I'd rather chew a menthol," Izzy says, tossing the balled-up gum wrapper out so it hits Dante's left boot.

Dante just stares at her.

"Just keeping it interesting," she says, and backs away

→ leaving us with Dante.

When she's gone he steps over to collect the mask, and, while he's down there, pinches that gum wrapper up from the asphalt as well, is about to lob it ahead of him into the trashcan but stops right at the release point.

He unballs it instead.

Close-up, framed by his massive hands, it's "*party @ Bo G's.*"

Dante smiles up at Izzy's retreating taillights, balls that gum wrapper back up smaller than it was, leaves it on top of the Billie Jean mask, grinning up from the trashcan.

Back in the video store after a contemplative beat, it's all harsh lights and customers pretending not to pay attention to what other customers are browsing .

Brittney's straightening the horror and thriller shelves all the way down to Jamie, who she's surprised is there. Her rapid blinking tells him so.

"Shouldn't you be at the local high school, I mean, *barbecue?*" she says.

Jamie flips the DVD he's got over to study the back.

It's *Intruder.*

"Too soon?" Brittney says, taking the DVD case, holding it down in front of her cleavage to scan it for him.

"What do you recommend?" Jamie asks, reaching across to pluck it back. She keeps it away, pulling his hand in dangerously close.

"Well what would you say you're looking for?" she asks, dropping *Intruder* into her apron.

"Up for anything," Jamie says, picking his words carefully. "Some comedy, some romance . . . "

"Melanie Griffith as a porn star?" Brittney asks, selecting *Body Double*, fake-reading from the back cover: "Supposed to be a sure ten on the peter meter."

"How old are you?" Jamie asks, guiding *Body Double* back.

"It was almost Jamie *Lee* Curtis," Brittney shrugs, about *Body Double*.

"What about zombies," Jamie says, reaching down for the obvious *Zombi*, one of three copies.

"Not really into the undead."

"But the way you were talking the other day."

"Oh but there's subgenres of subgenres in horror," Brittney says, pointing directly behind Jamie, where he just was. "Me, I'm more into the slasherific part of the shelf," she shrugs like a dare, brushing past him to put *Intruder* back in its place, which, lo and behold,

→ and close enough to see it but backed-off enough to take it all in, is an actual slasher section of the shelves, from *A Cat in the Brain* import and *Alone in the Dark* down to *When a Stranger Calls* and *Wrong Turn*, with VHSs of *X-Ray* and *You Better Watch Out* slipped in at the end. Back

→ up top—though no surprise, given how Brittney's directing Jamie that way—is a store tag reading *"courtesy Brittney,"* with a hand-drawn knife penetrating her name.

"No Z's?" Jamie says, still holding onto his *Zombi*.
"Rob Zombie got *Halloween*."
"Zebra Massacre? Zorro the, the Bloody Blade? Zoo something?"
"There's *Zodiac*"—reaching down to tap it, in Thriller—"but it's more serial killer, if that's what you're into."
"You tell me what I should be *into*," he says, catching her eye for a moment, in case the single entendre go unappreciated.
Brittney bites her lower lip deep into her mouth, pivots like a model at an auto show, and manages to bend down mostly in front of Jamie, come up with a battered VHS of *My Bloody Valentine*.
"It's a love story," she says, batting her eyes playfully.
"Sounds romantic," Jamie says, looking across to the front of the store, as if for Brittney's manager.
"There's a special promotion this week, too," Brittney says, reeling the video back, tucking it into her apron. "Home delivery for holiday-themed bodycount movies from the eighties—but only if they're Canadian. We're hoping to attract a very specific kind of customer, I guess."
"I do have a VCR I haven't used in a while."
"Those kind of units," Brittney says, "they need *constant* attention."
Jamie smiles.
"Still got that camera?" Brittney asks.
"Why?"
"Oh, no reason," Brittney says, practically flipping her skirt when she bounces away, except she's wearing pants.

Jamie gets the idea.

Also getting the idea is some tall, leery dude standing in the Adult section but peering across genres, watching all this. Putting it in the spank bank for later.

"Here," Jamie says to him, and flips *Driller Killer* up into his chest—fumble, fumble, catch—leaving us to wonder if he knows that movie or if this was just random, and we cut ahead a handful of minutes,

→ to that leery dude setting *Driller Killer* down at Brittney's register, his eyes all about her unbuttoned button.

She pushes the business card she was fondling back under the cash drawer, but not before we see a handwritten address.

"Name?" she says, fingers cocked over the keyboard, tracking from *Driller Killer* up to this dude then pulling her eyes away, looking past him, her POV tracking Jamie, ducking out the exit door

→ but the leery dude just smiles, watching her. Or, parts of her.

Surreptitiously, Brittney punches the manager assistance bell.

"Stay away from that camp . . . " the guy finally Crazy Ralphs out, smiling behind it, sure that he's found the magic key for the two of them, that's he making a connection.

"I'm doomed, right?" Brittney says, on autopilot here, still looking past this dude, the assistant manager approaching.

"How old *are* you?" the dude asks back, Brittney's POV on

→ Jamie again, retreating alongside the front windows of the video store, lobbing the cap from his just-bought coke at the trashcan.

It rims out.

He looks both ways like for witnesses. There aren't any, but still, good guy that he is, he ferrets the cap up from the parking curb, steps over to drop it into the trashcan, our POV suddenly *in* that trashcan, so we can look up from low enough to see Jamie's little chuckle of surprise at what's in there.

Or it could be satisfaction.

Or serendipity: there's a sword in play already.

Now there's a mask, too.

All we need to complete a holy trinity is

→ Mandy Kane some indefinite amount of time later. Long enough for it to be a lot darker, anyway, and the night has a feel like it's been in swing for a bit, as established by Mandy, standing from the open door of a car, her hair mussed, shirt untucked, some mellow smoke curling up around her.

She reaches back in for Jerry to hand her her barberpole tights and stands into them, snugging them up her thighs, her POV studying the posh house the party's going on at, the silhouette of some guy in a swimsuit running along a peak of the house, cannonballing off the backside

→ into a swimming pool, barely avoiding both the tiled edge of the pool *and* a guy floating on his back there like an otter, his beer on his chest.

The pool gulps the cannonballer in, the inevitable splash misting out across the various beer drinkers and hellraisers, not even one of them aware of a suspicious shape past the open gate of the fence around the backyard, in the turnrow of the corn field. A shape very possibly wearing a pale mask of some sort, and carrying something dull and heavy down by its right thigh.

The party mutes, becomes a

→ *heart*, beat; *heart*, beat

→ and we're close on this masked face, now—Billie Jean, hell yeah—his face now moving slightly, left to right, so his twin-eyehole POV can track a careless Lindsay working the crowd along the edge of the pool. She's in a sarong and bikini top and heeled sandals, all matching of course, her hair perfect, her smile even moreso.

"*Look, I'm moonwalking!*" somebody yells—probably while styling it off the roof—and Billie Jean's POV tears away from Lindsay, to

→ not Izzy, but we're in the car with her now, so who knows. Maybe he was *thinking* about her.

Izzy's smoking but having to hang her head out the window to do it. Because it's not her car.

What's coming through the stereo at high-volume is—get this—
"Just Like Jesse James."

Izzy's singing with Cher for all she's worth, drumming the dash,
shooting fake six-guns, smoking like a pool hustler. It all adds up to

→ her POV registering somebody standing in the road a moment
too late, so that, for the *second* time this night, a bumper of her
car nudges into that fingerswidth of loose jean fabric at somebody's
knees.

Except this somebody has to step back to keep it from being worse.
It's Ben.

He climbs into the passenger seat.

"You're smoking in her car," he says, still wet and not even slightly
happy, the grinder in his lap now, its battery light flashing yellow, the
blade spinning each time he taps the trigger.

"And you're sitting in her leather seat with wet clothes, Mr.
Haute Tension."

He shrugs, stabs a button on the radio, killing Jesse James taking
us right into "She's not There," just ramping up.

"What is this, oldies night?" he says, giving up, then, remembering: "You were there, weren't you? 'One school mascot please, and,
can you make it well-done this time?'"

"It wasn't funny."

"You love this stuff."

"I love it on video. You didn't see him."

"Accidents happen."

"Except this wasn't one."

"In your wet dreams."

"Just don't go down by the creek for a few days, okay?"

"It's not deep enough by our house anyway."

"Yeah, and I suppose my vodka just turns to water all on its own
down there?"

Ben doesn't acknowledge this.

"Promise?" Izzy insists.

"Tired of it anyway," Ben says. "Ready to graduate to bigger
shit. That high school's never going to know what hit it, when I get
there."

Izzy looks over to him, really evaluates him. Enough that she doesn't burst his bubble here.

He catches her watching him, scowls.

"So you think you're going to win the crown?" he says. "Get to be queen slut for the night?"

"That's Mom's job," Izzy says, and both of them kind of smile.

"But no, I don't have a chance in hell. Dad's my date, you know?"

"Serious?"

"As the heart attack he's working up to."

Ben nods, considering this. Staring straight ahead, their shared POV showing the metal sculptures of their house taking shape in the headlights.

"You're not coming back again after graduation, are you?" Ben says, our angle on him through the side glass, so we can see what he's hiding: that he's actually kind of serious, here. And absolutely terrified.

"Why would I?" Izzy answers back, then wishes she could reel it back in. "I mean, I guess I'll have to, to play good aunt to all the little Bens you'll be fathering your sophomore year, right?"

"Me neither," he says, still looking out the window. "I'm never coming back here. No matter what she says."

"Come live with me," Izzy says, waiting for the garage door to reel itself up. "Me and Brittney are going to have this rocking apartment, and go to concerts all the time, and date tattoo artists to get free ink. I'm sure there'll be a high school near."

"I'm going to be in the basement," Ben says, standing all at once from the car, before they're even in the garage.

Izzy watches him walk through the headlights into the house, and dials the volume down on the radio, looks down the slope behind their house, so that her imaginary POV is tunneling down through the brush and darkness, hurtling towards the creek and what we know's there, under a blanket of fake leaves:

→ a red-rimmed eye, slamming open.

Back to Izzy's face, breathing deep on her cigarette, the car still idling in front of the empty garage.

A hand reaches around her neck, plucks her cigarette, drops it.

Mom.

Izzy sits up straighter, looks ahead, into the garage.

Her dad's there, barefoot in a poorly-fitting suit, drink in hand.

"Thought we were doing wardrobe rehearsal tonight?" Izzy's mom says, opening the door.

Izzy's POV looks down to the brake and the gas pedal, side by side, so easy, then up to her father, just standing there drunk and stupid, and all we can hear is her breathing, and, in that, her deliberation.

She finally kills the car, steps up from it.

"This should be fun," she says, and, before following her mom inside, she stops to grind out the cigarette on the driveway, look around one last time, her POV suspecting . . . a shape in the trees?

Either way, she walks backwards into the garage, then brings the door down between her and us, so that at the end she's just combat boots.

Then nothing.

The wind whistles through the metal sculptures of her dark house, and the cigarette she ground out, it glows back on and we're right on top of it, as if curious that this can happen, though we're also not sure if we're a lumbering POV or not.

A jarring cut later—lost in darkness, like that cigarette died—we're looking through a video camera at the out-of-control party out in the spooky corn fields.

We're not in the corn, though, but are following some girl's ass, her skirt not that long, her heels uselessly tall.

And, that girl?

She feels this attention, turns around: it's April, her hair down, her clothes not at all her usual nerdware, the

→ cameraman complimenting her with a "*Sa-andy*," doing the Travolta shock down to his knees.

It's Davis, from English class.

"Got that right, stud," April says, and drops an imaginary cigarette, looks away like it's hot and she's bored, her hand coming over like the most natural thing, to unbutton the top button of her too-tight blouse.

The camera'd POV zooms back in, drawing closer to this action, closer, finally close enough that April can lean forward, plant a fat sloppy kiss right on the lens, smearing the already unfocused image of her, so we pull back to

→ "*Shit*, April!" Davis is saying, pulling his camera down "I thought you were cool now?"

"Really?" she says, taking this insult in stride. "I never thought you were," and when Lindsay walks by, hugging April's shoulder in some 'sisterly,' 'hopeful' way we go with her, kind of drop into her

→ privileged POV, so we can see the party's reaction to her: they all love her, want to be next to her, want to be seen by her, are glad just to go to the same high school as her.

"Final girl high five!" some guy yells, and April touches her palm to his.

"Michael Jordan sucks!" another says, but somebody punches him in the chest, says, "Michael Jackson, ass hat."

Another walks backwards in front of her, singing, "*I always feel like, somebody's wa-atching me . . .*" which cues up that song's intro synth, either on the stereo system or the soundtrack, it's hard to tell, but it goes unnaturally long before the lyrics start, long enough for

→ Mandy to ask, "Where's Jake?" her make-up fry-daddied, her eyes mellow yellow.

"Home for his beauty rest," Lindsay says, shrugging. "Doctor's orders . . . don't want tomorrow night to be anything less than perfect, do we? And"—Lindsay adds, reaching across to touch up Mandy's face—"is this really the image we want to project, you think, or . . . surely it's not a tactic to appeal for votes, is it?"

"Ballot boxes are locked in the school," Jerry says.

Lindsay appraises Jerry, her face calm and tolerant, and she looks calmly away, a practiced gesture, it seems,

→ her aloof POV settling on Crystal over by the pool, talking to some Ponyboy of an underwear model, reaching across to guide her long hair over her shoulder, out of the way. She's in shorts that would make Catherine Bach blush, an almost long enough white t-shirt, and old brown cowboy boots, making beautiful such a casual affair

→ that she—Lindsay—is about to eviscerate Jerry with words, it looks like, when he's saved by a wall of water rising from the pool, everybody there recording this with their phones, Lindsay screeching away.

"*I can't get my arm wet!*" she screams, but it's lost, and then the Rockwell cues up properly as we pan out to the corn field again, no shape there anymore. Just menace.

Back *in* the backyard, one of the refugee football players shucks his shirt, shields Lindsay back towards the dryness of the patio just as a rumbling sifts down over the party.

Not thunder . . . footsteps?

Yep: a lineman absolutely *launches* off that last eave of the house, still pedaling even in the air, like he's going to need every inch of distance he can coax out of this jump.

It's nothing new for this party, except, this time, he's cradling a bikini-clad girl in his arms, and the way she's writhing against him, it's not exactly helping their balance.

People scream, fall back, but the two suicides make it, somehow.

More than that: the lineman comes up with the girl's bikini top in his teeth, shakes it in his mouth, everybody close enough pouring their beer onto the monster he now officially is, the topless, holding-herself girl getting some of that fountain action herself.

"Talk about *Gorillas in the Mist*," April says, her new and brave outfit evidently not working the magic she thought it was going to. We can tell because she's nervously braiding her hair back into pigtails.

But maybe it *is* working?

A football player is suddenly running toward her, scooping her onto his shoulder, running for the half wall that leads up onto the roof, but

→ close-up and in jangling motion, we see her hiking her already short skirt up to the danger zone, reaching in and

→ leaning back in this football player's two-arm hug, a small-caliber pistol right in his face, both her arms behind it like she's on the range.

"Whoah, January, June, Ms. September, whatever," he says, setting her down gently.

"It's April," April says. "But thanks for the effort."

She watches him back off, hikes her dress back up to snug the pistol high on her thigh.

"My father calls it a chastity belt," she says, snapping the garter holding the pistol up. "What do you think?"

"We're just having fun," the football player says, his hands still up, fully in view. "Listen, I've got a game tomorrow, you know? And—and *my* dad, if I don't get to play, he'll—"

"Go," April says, waving his boring self away, already looking somewhere else:

→ at Lindsay, studying her.

Lindsay raises her good hand to the one in the sling, gives April a polite golf clap, though the way she's biting her bottom lip, she's not just completely in approval here.

"Gonna make a great nun-slash-assassin someday," a thicknecked rich boy says, sidled up next to April somehow.

April turns, evaluates him and his friend, the friend shirtless and in charge in a way that means this is his party. It's the kind of swagger a young Brad Wesley could pull off without trying: days spent on the links, nights spent in hot tubs, wine with dinner, and dinner lasts for hours.

"Bogey," April says, naming him for us.

"You got a, you know, a *permit* for a weapon that dangerous?" Bogey says, pointing to her skirt with his mixed drink hand.

"You gonna take it away from me?" April says.

"I just might at that," Bogey says, April never even for an instant breaking eye contact with him, at which point glass breaks offscreen and an octopus shadow passes across the pebbled cement, screaming the whole way, a bikini top drifting down.

A few steps away, Jerry plucks that top from the air, gets what's probably his trademark evil grin, and passes it to Mandy, who slides it through her left sleeve hole, settles it in place then lifts her arms for Jerry to shimmy her top off.

She turns around, kissing him deep as her nimble fingers tie the bikini string behind her back.

Close-up on their mouths, both kissing and speaking.
Mandy: "Is she watching?"
Jerry's POV ratchets around so as to keep this kiss going.
He finds Lindsay, sneering.
"Screw her," he says right into Mandy's mouth, and

→ we're looking at her back, can see her quit tying her top, the strings dangling now, everybody around the pool chanting for them to take it farther, meaning none of them are aware of the dim outline of Billie Jean, standing ominous and judgmental up on that launching pad of an eave above them all.

Just watching. A sword rising in silhouette from his middle.

The song coming on strong now, definitely from the house speakers, is "Let the Bodies Hit the Floor."

Of course.

First, though, a fast series:

→ Brittney walking out the front of the video store, a VHS clamshell in her hand, her apron folded over her arm, that business card in her other hand.

She stops just past the sidewalk, looks up the street, then the other way;

→ Izzy standing on a chair in her kitchen, her mother pinning a frilly dress up all around her, Izzy's eyes completely somewhere else;

→ Ben in the basement by the red-hot furnace, beating another piece of metal into shape;

→ Dante's car nosed up to some of those football players in the ditch, a stop sign bent under the front of their car, their car slid up it a bit, Dante not paying attention at all, his POV settled on the party house in the distance, across all that corn silk, all those swaying tassels rushing beneath us so that we're

→ already *at* the house, upstairs in the master bedroom.

It's mostly dark, just outlines.

And the sounds of two people finding each other in the king bed.

"No, no, I like your hair like that," Bogey says.

"But my skirt—"

"Keep it on."

"Well then. Study hard."

"I never knew."

"Are you—are you on the ballot?"

"Is that like being in the box?"

"Umm, close enough."

"You bring any, yeah, um, yeah . . . protection?"

"This work?" and we hear the distinct, very naughty click of a gun's hammer.

Bogey chuckles, his mouth too occupied for words anymore, their fumbling shapes backlit for a moment by the huge window by the bed, and we

→ get a different angle on them.

This one through a pair of eyeholes. Eyeholes that tilt over about twenty degrees, for a better angle.

Those eyeholes look down to the long black sword in Billie Jean's hand. The long black sword with the raw silver edge.

When the motion on the bed stops for a moment, April maybe looking across the room, *into* these eyeholes,

→ those eyeholes step back and sideways, into the huge bathroom.

The lights in here have been dimmed. In passing the wide mirror above the twin sinks, Billie Jean catches his reflection, turns to study it, trying to get that Hodder head tilt just right. Then he raises the sword slow by his side, like trying to show off his bicep, even though it's buried in the blue sleeve of mechanic coveralls.

Rounding the corner of this bathroom, then—it's spacious enough to have corners—Billie Jean stops to study a girl passed out on the floor, by the toilet, cherry vomit sprayed over its side.

That black sword reaches down, nudges her, and then there's a sound in the shower.

Billie Jean's POV backs off, the sword springing up.

Nothing, nothing.

More hot and heavy breathing.

Billie Jean steps over, getting the dim light behind him, and chocks his hand up on the sword so that, in shadow, it's a knife.

He *Psycho*s it on the shower curtain, the violin tracing the movements in case we're somehow not getting it, but then something in the master bedroom shatters in a blue flash.

From the other side of the bed, like looking in through the window if the window wasn't there, Bogey's saying, "Don't worry about it, don't worry about it"—the lamp—and we can see one of April's hands squeezing onto one of the poles of this four poster, the whole thing rocking hard, nearly as loud as their almost-there almost-there breathing.

Back in the monstrous bathroom, Billie Jean reaches up, tears down the halogen-white shower curtain, and it's just as easy as it always is in the movies.

It's two guys in there, all over each other.

They fall back, seeing Billie Jean, but he just stares at them, finally turning his head once to the left, for them to leave.

Tiptoeing past the passed-out girl, they do, holding hands.

Billie Jean's POV looks down on this passed-out girl. He turns her over.

Carefully so as not to wake her, he removes her cat-eye glasses, sets her head back on the tile, into her vomit, and, moving slowly, he removes her belt as well

→ just as the butt of a mag-lite knocks on the front door of Bogey's house.

It's Dante.

There's a sock on the doorknob.

Dante sneers, knocks harder.

Back to the master bed, the ceiling above it shuddering with thunder—another couple launching off into space.

Moments later, that splash, the screams of being alive, a chant of "Take it off! Take it off!"

"Again," April says in the darkness, her face glistening, her POV cueing in slowly to something in the open doorway to the bathroom.

It's a ghost. With glasses. A belt around its neck.

She pushes back, into the headboard, and

→ Bogey sits up, turns that way and chuckles appreciation.

"All right," he says. "We're terrified, aghhh," and he stands on the bed, "come over here, though, I got something to show—"

His POV interrupts, though: he's stood tall enough that he's in the fan's space, those blades *whipping* around at top speed.

One of them catches him perfectly on the bridge of the nose, launching him backwards, and we're backed off enough that we can see it all in slow-motion:

→ his body, arcing back, leading with the head;

→ April, looking over to where he's going now, which should be the window, but it is

→ Billie Jean, standing there with his sword jutting out from the hip.

Bogey impales himself on that sword with a distinct crunch, its black tip erupting from his lower stomach in a splash of blood, Billie Jean stepping back in surprise, jerking his masked face over to April, who's falling back, away from this, thunder resounding down from above,

→ her little pistol firing again and again

→ into Billie Jean's chest.

He paws at those craters of fabric opening up on the front of his jumpsuit, still hanging onto the sword somehow, and one of those shots misses, shatters through the glass

→ whips perfectly into Mandy Kane's left eye as she flies through the air, cradled by Jerry.

The force of the shot jerks her head back, spins Jerry in the air— they're both naked except for her tights—and he drops her, has to push away from her in the air

→ just as Billie Jean is crashing back through that master bedroom window, falling in slow motion to the square shrubs below.

Jerry comes down hard and awkward, his open mouth catching the lip of the far side of the pool for one last, especially deep kiss: it forces his chin down, his face up, curbing him Edward Norton style, and, because he's naked,

→ underwater and from the side, too fast and bubbly for any real frontal nudity but we get the idea, his crotch slams into one of those sealed lights built into the side of the pool, and his last act is to penetrate that light's glass cover.

The jolt of electricity kicks his head back, but, since he's still connected to the light, it slams his face forward again, into the edge, splitting his jaw all the way back to the ears, everybody screaming.

Because of the short he's creating, then,

→ all the lights go black.

Deputy Dante splinters through the door, his mag-lite cocked over his service revolver like we've all seen a hundred times.

Upstairs, he hears something break, but first he stops, listens, jerks the closet door open.

It's those two guys from the shower, holding each other.

"Get the hell out of here," he says, ushering them behind him, while

→ in the backyard, everybody's vaulting the cinderblock fence, crashing into the corn field at top speed, absolutely blind,

→ one of their POVs racing down a row, corn grabbing at them everywhere, and it's a football player, we can tell by the breathing

→ and by how hard he tries to tackle the tractor tire he slams into.

He falls back unconscious, and Lindsay kneels over him, looks behind her, drags him under the tractor, and all we see is her cell phone glowing with emergency.

Back at the house, Dante steps into the backyard, shines his light out across the water.

There's Jerry, *so* dead.

Crumpled on the tile just short of the pool is Mandy, dead as well, if not deader. Like a wet pretzel that fell from an airplane. A pretzel filled with jelly.

"Shit," Dante says, and steps

→ onto the second floor, still leading with his light.

He cases the bedroom, finds only dolls, studies the next room which is a painting studio, mostly Corvettes in oil, then eases into the master bath,

→ his hand feeling for the passed-out girl's pulse.

It's there.

He takes the flashlight from beneath his chin, stands from her, steps through the second bathroom door, into the master bedroom.

His light finds Bogey, the bed soaked black with his blood.

"Shit," Dante says again, and whips the light away, realizing the window's crashed through.

Reversed on him now, so we can see the room behind him, the fake ghost rises, stands, its eyeholes all misaligned. But still, this ghost levels something at him under the shower curtain. It starts at the waist, comes up to about mid-chest.

Dante feels this with his Spidey sense, stops moving, angles his head back and dives just as a shot cuts across where he just was, the slug whipping out through the window,

→ shattering the glass of the tractor Lindsay's huddled under.

The glass rains down around her and she just glares at it, her phone still glowing at the side of her head.

We get back to the bedroom just as that ghost whips through the doorway, the jamb exploding from two of Dante's shots.

Now's where Wes does some scary shit, all through the house, cat and mouse, this ghost versus this cop, until, finally, the ghost stabs April's hand out to the counter by the fridge, comes back with a serious ring of keys, fobs all over it.

More important, a garage-door opener.

April slithers to the sliding door that opens onto the backyard and pushes the garage-door opener, that grinding sound pulling Dante away, who was velociraptoring it up just above the counter she's ducked under.

He runs one way, she runs the other

→ ghosting through the backyard

→ getting over the fence like it's nothing,

→ stripping the shower curtain off as she runs through the corn, trying to get her bra on at full-tilt,

→ flashing by the tractor, which is curiously not a shelter for anybody anymore

→ angling into another row when she sees cell phone glow ahead of her

→ ditching her pistol in the dirt, meaning she's just about

→ home free, has been saved by her wits, has had sex and got away clean.

Except for the blade slicing out of the row beside her now

We only hear the sickening sound of it,

→ come back in her POV, looking up, dying, a shape stepping into her field of vision

→ but now we're on her face, so calm, so serene.

"Seriously?" she says, as if completely disgusted by who this is, then the blade we still haven't seen goes deeper

→ sends us back to the master bedroom, Dante standing on the bedroom-side of that shattered window, surveying the damage.

"Gonna need a bigger boat," he finally says, and looks down for whatever fell from here.

The ground below is that Haddonfield kind of empty. Just shattered glass, which we

→ tunnel down into and back out of, speeder-biking it out of control across the top of all this corn to a scarecrow way out there in the morning light, and that scarecrow, it's April, most of her insides on the outside, the music shrieking about it.

Packed in the cab of the tractor a few rows over from her, the sun just touching them, are ten or twelve of the kids from the party, the rest of them hugging themselves and each other on the plow, except for Lindsay.

She's sitting out on the hood, the dust on her face streaked with tears.

She looks down to her phone

→ and its Izzy's cracked display, Izzy's fingers gripping it.

She's sleeping, the phone in her hand.

It shakes and gives a sick beep, does it again, and finally she reaches her other hand up to it, hits the right button

→ pulls it under the covers, close to her face, her POV not making sense of anything at first.

Slowly it comes into focus, though: "*hey, lover.*"

She rolls over, clears the blankets from her face, sits up blinking. Looks to the phone again, menus up to the callback number, which she highlights, calls.

"Who is this?" she says.

"Just wanted to say thanks."

A girl.

Lindsay?

"Crystal?" Izzy guesses, instead.

"Thanks for springing me, I mean."

"I probably don't know what you're talking about."

Crystal laughs, switches ears it sounds like.

"You mean you're sleeping?"

"No school."

"I mean after last night."

Izzy's POV settles on the pink cupcake of a dress hanging on her closet door.

"It was hell, yeah," she says, rolling over, away from the sight of it.

"Seen the video yet?" Crystal asks.

"Video?"

"I'll send a link. It's already on the news, too."

"Shit," sitting up hard. "Something happened."

"Party of the year, horror girl. But hey, we're even after this, okay?"

"After what?"

"That *Walking Tall* deputy?"

"Series or the remake?"

"Scratch that. That deputy from *Heat of the Night?* What was his name—Bubba?"

"What are you saying, Crystal?"

"Dante,"

→ which takes us to Crystal, face-on at first but we swing around behind her, to see what she's seeing: Dante's car at a fancy house.

"He's across the street from me right now."

"Across the . . . " Izzy says, then gets it, and it's bad enough we have to go all the way back to her face for her to say it: "*Brittney.*"

And she's flying out of bed,

→ screeching from the garage

→ fishtailing around a corner, her not-driving hand punching hard on the link Crystal's just shot across.

It opens a video of two naked forms hurtling off a roof in a slow pirouette, blood slinging away from them, and then, circled in the dim background and slowed down, Billie Jean crashing from a window, onto the ground.

Izzy slides to a stop halfway up the curb of what must be Brittney's house, just a street or two over.

Crystal's sitting on the hood of a car across the street, phone in hand, hair down and eyes sleepy, a wicked grin on her face—an Ariel Moore for the new century—the house behind her magnificent, opulent, decadent.

"What is it?" Izzy yells to her. "Is she—did something happen to her?"

Before Crystal can shrug either a no-answer or an I-don't-care, it's hard to tell with her and her bedroom eyes, Izzy's running across the lawn

→ right into Dante's chest.

He keeps her from falling, and then she starts hitting him with everything she's got.

"You were supposed to keep them safe!" she screams. "You're supposed to keep shit like this from happening! I thought we were on the same side!"

Dante has no response, just takes her punches, finally pulls her into a hug, patting the back of her head.

Izzy collapses, crying into his shirt.

"Not her," she's saying, now. "Not her."

She pushes away from Dante.

"What happened?" she says, the anger back in her voice, her face. "Can I see her at least?"

Dante rolls his John Deere-green toothpick, takes it out, inserts it back in butt-first.

"She wasn't at the party," he says. "She never made it home from work last night, evidently."

"It was Billie Jean," Crystal calls across, thrilled. "I saw him!"

Izzy looks up to Dante about this and he nods.

"I saw the video," Izzy says, pushing him except he's solid enough it only pushes her back. "It's somebody in a Billie Jean *mask*."

Dante narrows his eyes down at her about this.

"It wasn't him," Izzy says, then sees who must be Brittney's yoga mom step out onto the lawn.

Izzy runs over, hugs her, ends up just holding both her hands, looking into her eyes.

"We hoped she was with you," the mom says.

"We split up," Izzy says, letting the mom's hands go. Looking through the front door of Brittney's house,

→ stepping into Brittney's bedroom, Dante hulking behind her.

On the walls are collages of Brittney and Izzy from the last year. Izzy touches one of them with her fingertips as if seeing them for the first time.

"You're thinking," Izzy says back to Dante, collecting her voice for this, "you're thinking she's a die-hard horror fan, didn't want the action to stop, so she put a mask on last night, went to the party, made her own movie."

"If she were here I could clear her," Dante says.

"If she were here, I could punch her," Izzy says, and walks across to the walk-in closet,

→ ducks inside, clicking the light on.

It's rows and rows of clothes.

Izzy glides her fingers along the shoulders of the blouses and dresses, finally pulls out a grey one with vague red accents.

"Is this evidence?" she says back to Dante. "I can take another if it is."

"What did you mean it wasn't Billie Jean. Twenty people recorded it."

Izzy looks over to him, then to Brittney's mom standing in the doorway, her eyes swollen and red.

"Think maybe you should come with me," Izzy says, and the next time we see her

→ she's in the back of Dante's deputy cruiser, staring out with the blankest look, the dress hanging on the other side of the backseat from her.

"It's over," she says to herself, her POV now seeing all the helicopters hovering two or three miles out like flies over a carcass.

Dante readjusts his rearview to see her better.

"She took a movie home, if that means anything," he says. "A videotape."

"She didn't go home," Izzy says. "That reporter. She was talking to him when I was talking to you, last night."

"Reporter?"

"You brought him to school yesterday."

" . . . Leslie, Casey—*Jackie*?"

"Sam, Chris, Pat, Max?" Izzy adds. "Tracy, Shannon, Dana Carvey?"

"What?"

"Jamie. Jamie Curtis. The 'Lee' is silent."

"She was in *Blue Steel*, right?"

"Best slasher that never was."

"Never was what?"

"Known as a slasher."

"You're really into this movie stuff, aren't you?" Dante asks.

"Movies are the world, and I live in the world, yeah. You too, Blue Steel."

"And she was into them like you? Britt?"

"She doesn't like to be called that," Izzy says. "That's a boy's name." She winces then, to have said it, to have made her a Ripley, a Sidney. "You did that on purpose, didn't you?"

"That horror movie she took home, it was . . . " Dante says, working a flip pad up from his chest pocket to read from it, "*My Bloody Valentine*?"

"Love story. Figures. Old one or new?"

"It matter?"

"She liked the old one," Izzy says, staring out the window again, then squints in pain, corrects herself: "*Likes*, I mean. She likes the old one. She likes it now, wherever she is, and she'll like it later, when this is all over and done with."

Dante studies her in the rearview again.

Izzy looks right up into his eyes.

"If homecoming wasn't tonight, I might could bait him in for you," she says. "The fake Billie Jean. I mean, not me, obviously, but whoever he really wants. Whoever this is all really for. Whoever's worthy."

"Lindsay."

"Probably."

"Doesn't matter. Homecoming isn't tonight anymore."

"It has to be," Izzy says. "It's what he or she or they've been waiting for, planning around. Last night was foreplay. Tonight's the money shot."

"Billie Jean isn't real," Dante says, taking a turn especially slow, as if Izzy is that fragile. "It's just Brooks Baker off his rocker, getting high off his own supply, playing Halloween. And I've got him in lockdown already."

"Lindsay's dad's actually named Brooke?"

"Brooks. As in creek, plural."

Izzy laughs about this without smiling, and a cut later

→ they're crunching down through the trees and leaves behind Izzy's house, towards the creek.

On the way, Izzy looks up to the house, sees her brother framed in his upstairs window, watching them, his arms black with ash and work, his face smudged.

"Well," Dante says then, and stops, clears the leaf litter away from

→ the sheriff's glinting badge.

"Hunh," Izzy says, just walking past, not impressed.

Dante uses his pen to balance the badge up into his jacket pocket then follows Izzy, his eyes different now, but not different enough for his POV to catch Ben up in his window, even though it seems like his shadow's still there. Or the ash he was wearing. Or his ghost.

And then they're at the creek, Izzy and Dante, each of them breathing hard. A crisp, shiny morning.

"I shouldn't have done it," Izzy says. "You don't have to lecture me. I should have called him in, I know."

"You talking about the sheriff?" Dante says.

"I'm talking about him," Izzy says, pulling hard on the yellow cord, the music climbing, a section of the leaves shifting away to show . . .

Nothing. Silence.

Izzy can't process this.

"What?" Dante's saying, stepping in beside her. "Your dad's old turkey hunting blind?"

Dante reaches down to shake it all the way free.

It's just a blind. Burrito wrappers all in it. And a smell that makes him cover his nose with the back of his hand.

"He's wearing a leg brace," Izzy finally says. "The real Billie Jean. That's how you'll know. When we get to the Scooby-Doo part and there's two of them, that's how you'll be able to tell."

Dante's watching her.

"Or just shoot them both if you want," Izzy adds, shrugging all his unasked questions off. "They both deserve it."

Dante extracts the badge from his jacket with a tissue, hooks it on the rough bark of the big tree.

"I'm going to have to tape off this whole area," he says, looking back up the steep slope.

"This whole town," Izzy corrects, and he looks to her but she's just studying the shimmering surface of the water, her face slack, only looking up

→ as if in response to the sudden sound of brakes hissing.

It's a school bus, rolling into Danforth High School's trash-strewn parking lot. The bus's windows are shoe-polished with *Beat the Titans* and *Release the Kraken* kind of stuff.

Behind the bus is a parade of decorated cars.

The bus stops before the main entrance, a tennis shoe stepping down onto the asphalt.

We back off slow and the polyester shorts and tucked-in gold shirt ID this as a coach, and the paunch says *head* coach, and, by the time we finally make it to this coach's head he's turned away from us, studying this big emptiness, trying to make sense of it, so all we can see is some salt and pepper hair.

But then he reaches up, peels his hat off to scratch his scalp with a pinky and turns around so casual, squinting against the sun.

Robert Englund.

Hell yes.

An instant later

→ he's shaking the chained front doors.

Nobody answers.

He scowls, cups his hands around his eyes, peers in through the glass, his POV able to make out the trophy case.

The sword's still there.

"They turn tail when they heard it was us?" a deep voice asks, and

→ we reverse, look up, and up.

Tony Todd.

The Bulldogs' coach is Freddy Krueger, their assistant coach the Candyman.

"We never had a chance, did we?" Izzy says to Dante over the top of Dante's cruiser.

"Don't call it yet," Dante says, opening his door, his hand reaching in for a big roll of police tape, his police radio crackling to life.

"What now?" he says, sitting sideways in the front seat, holding the radio mike to his mouth.

"You might want to get over here," the woman deputy says, and he gingerly sets the mike back in its place

→ is already pulling into the parking lot of the high school, driving slow like this is a trap, Izzy in the front seat beside him, the roll of yellow tape in her lap, her fingers pulling at the leading edge of it, her POV tracking the female deputy's car, already cocked at an angle in front of the bus.

Sitting in the back of it, watching Izzy back, is Lindsay, locked up safe just like Dante said.

Her eyes are puffy and red, her face washed out, no make-up.

She blinks hopefully across the parking lot to Izzy, puts her hand to her bulletproof glass, and Izzy looks purposefully away,

→ to some of the Bulldogs out on the field, running drills in half pads on their own, because

→ their coaches are under the overhang sheltering the main doors of the school.

With Dante.

"I'm sorry you came all this way, Coach," Dante's saying. "Maybe you should have tuned in some news."

"We left at five," the assistant coach says. "No cell phones on the bus. It's policy."

"Even for us," the head coach adds, pushing away from the wall, watching his boys out on the field, a cheerleader just past them launching up into the air, towards our skybound POV, then falling back, but we don't get to see her get caught, are

→ back at the school.

"We can spot you however many players you need, Deputy," the head coach is saying. "First stringers, even, keep it fair."

Dante looks away, to Izzy, walking from his cruiser to the other one.

Izzy sits down in the front seat, adjusts the rearview to center Lindsay in it.

"And then there were three," Izzy says.

"What?" Lindsay says.

"You were there," Izzy says.

"Which time?" Lindsay says, sobbing a little smile.

"They're deciding whether tonight's grindhouse double feature'll happen or not."

Izzy stares at Lindsay in the mirror.

"What are you wanting out of it all?" Izzy says.

Lindsay dabs the corner of her eye in that way that means she doesn't want wrinkles, shakes her head no.

"I just want it to be over," she says. "For all—all my friends to be . . . "

"Ditto," Izzy says, her POV settling on Dante and the assistant coach, in each other's faces now, their voices obviously getting raised.

"Who you think would win?" Izzy says, about the two giants, squaring off.

"It's all my fault, right?" Lindsay says, coming up to the wire separator.

Izzy turns around so they're face-to-face, Izzy's eyes hot, her left hand using the upright shotgun for support, the slide racking back by accident.

She doesn't look over to it. Just at Lindsay.

"It's *my* dad," Lindsay whispers. "I mean, it's not him anymore, he could never—but it's him. I should, I should just—"

"Let the villagers Fay Wray you out at the edge of town?" Izzy smiles. "Maybe, yeah. But not yet."

Lindsay cocks her head, doesn't follow.

"Unless it does turn out to be you, of course," Izzy adds. "Then I'll spit on your grave myself. Take you to the last house on the left just before dawn."

Lindsay presses the heel of her hand between her eyes for a long moment, finally comes back up with "I'm guessing that's a clever threat of some sort?"

"You knew who Jason Voorhees's mom was," Izzy says.

"And—and that means I'm choreographing all my friends *dying*? You know what? I know who Krusty the Clown is too, does that mean I'm a cartoon? Do animated characters find their fathers stomped nearly to death in a stall? Do cartoon people have to go to six funerals in one *week*? Do their horses get blinded in *sword*fights, by Michael Jackson? Just because you and your little friend light candles for serial killers, don't think the rest of us do, okay? I was giving you a chance, with homecoming. I thought you deserved it. That it might get you back on the path. That you might be somebody. You've got it in you, you know?"

Izzy just stares at her until she looks away.

"I don't even want to be, to be queen anymore," she says, almost sobbing.

"Crown hanging heavy?" Izzy offers.

"Cute. Shakespeare?"

"Think it's Conan," Izzy says, pushing her unholy cell phone back through the wire.

Lindsay catches it, doesn't know what to do with it.

"My little friend, she remembers you from third grade," Izzy says.

Lindsay closes her eyes, is crying now.

"And she's MIA right now too."

Lindsay looks up about this, says, "Last night?"

"The longer she's missing, the more likely she's not coming back," Izzy adds, speaking forward now, her hands at ten and two on the wheel. "We need to get to the third reel of this before somebody goes all *Hostel* on her, understand?"

"Third reel?" Lindsay says.

"The big game," Izzy explains. "The big dance. The end of all this."

"Homecoming."

"My last chance to be somebody, yeah," Izzy says. "Now, get your mom on the phone. Who can say no to an almost widow?"

"She's a councilwoman too," Lindsay says, dialing, blinking, sniffling in then dialing some more.

"All the better. Any chance Crystal's dad is too?"

Next is Dante, whipping Izzy's battered cell phone away from the side of his head. Like pulling a scab. Izzy and Lindsay leaning on the deputy's car behind him, their arms crossed.

Dante looks up slow and grim, to the players and cheerleaders watching him through the white letters of their windows. Waiting.

He nods once to them: okay.

Out on the field, the quarterback, who can hear the cheering from the bus, nods, steps back to punt the ball in pure, unadulterated joy, *blasting* it up into the sky, so it hangs, hangs, hangs some more, and somewhere under that perfect spiral punt, a montage is going on, complete with gearing-up music:

→ Crystal's swank, mob-lawyer dad setting his phone back down on its cradle, nodding once to Crystal, standing in the doorway;

→ a helmet being snugged down hard onto some player's head;

→ a 1972 ragtop Cadillac easing up the packed red clay of the track around the football field, the Cadillac all ticker-taped out for the big halftime show, Mrs. Graves behind the wheel

→ her POV studying the gathering clouds;

→ Izzy's mom in the living room, dancing with the dress she's chosen for Izzy;

→ Dante, opening the gun safe at the Sheriff's offices, passing shotguns back to other officers;

→ the assistant coach's hands slamming down on a player's shoulder pads in that way coaches do, when they won't hug;

→ Lindsay, stepping out of the back of the deputy's cruiser and into an exclusive hair salon, somebody already holding the door for her;

→ Izzy in Brittney's bedroom, one of those bulletin-board photo collages in her lap;

→ Ben in the basement wearing a welding helmet, whatever he's doing glowing in the dark glass he's looking through;

→ the Bulldog cheerleaders, circling their upper arms with simple black ribbon;

→ the creek, purling gently past, a few raindrops splattering into its surface;

→ somebody in a light raincoat laying down chalk lines on the football field, the wind pulling at his clothes;

→ Dante, walking out of a bathroom with the newspaper and a small, still-wet key;

→ a bunch of football players praying on one knee in a locker room;

→ that Cadillac, just sitting there in front of the empty stands, it's top up against the thunder reverberating all around;

→ Izzy's mom putting a bottle back into the liquor cabinet and wiping her mouth, then reaching in for one more slosh, *then* pushing the door shut, inserting the key, snapping it cleanly off and kissing the part she still has, for luck;

→ Crystal's locker in the dark high school, her homecoming'd photo on front X'd out;

→ the cliff Billie Jean fell from, nobody there;

→ a deputy's cruiser parked outside Brittney's house, the woman deputy leaning against the side of the car, waiting;

→ Izzy, standing in what's obviously Brittney's bathroom, an X of eyeliner already dragged across her face in the mirror. She looks at herself through it for a beat or two more then down to what-all beauty supplies Brittney has;

→ her hand reaching down through this dream, for a hair brush;

→ a different hand taking that wall-mounted sword by the handle;

→ dusk settling over things, the stadium lights glowing on through the drizzle, and we stay there in that nostalgic moment.
Just another Friday night in small-town America.
At least until

→ we go tight on a horse's whiskery nostrils in some kind of tight darkness.
They blow hard and mad, startle us up in our seats.
This is it.

ACT 3

Helmets slam into each other silently in the rain, and then the sound catches up all at once.

The game. Titans defending homecoming against the Bulldogs. Rivershead showing the world that it's not dead, that it's not giving up.

We go from the visiting head coach's face, looking away from the rest of the play like it hurts him

→ to the Bulldog cheerleaders, soaking wet but cheering on the home side, right in front of the Cadillac, their faces intensely happy, their movements precise

→ the packed stands above them clapping, insisting on the happiness of tonight. A sea of umbrellas and tarps, everybody up there desperate to ignore

→ the respectful pan across all the framed portraits stood up at the inside curb of the track, right before the field starts.

Some of these school photos have empty helmets in front of them. Five others, pom-poms—why the Bulldog cheerleaders are working the Titan stands, probably.

One photo, Mandy's, has a nicely folded pair of red and white tights, a rose laid across them, the rain beading off it.

Jerry's has a football helmet and a full bottle of beer.

Those helmets slam together again, the sound there this time like it should be, violent and delicate at the same time, with the same crash.

One of the players doesn't get up from the mud.

We angle up on the crowd, silent now, standing, hands over their hearts, the cheerleaders all taking a knee,

→ one dad in particular standing up at the front rail like he's either about to jump over or run the other way, a woman at his arm, holding it tight, keeping him there, and then comes a voiceover, a girl we maybe know, reciting lines:

> "*Their sons grow suicidally beautiful*
> *At the beginning of October,*
> *And gallop terribly against each other's bodies.*"

Up in the empty side of the announcer's booth, we can see that hurt player through the wet glass, but are having to look through three reflected faces to do it: Izzy, Lindsay, Crystal.

We can't see their dresses, not even really their hair.

Izzy turns her reflection over to Crystal, says, impressed, "Did you just make that up?"

"AP English," Lindsay says, keeping her eyes straight ahead.

"Pleasance?" Izzy asks.

"He lets us grade y'all's papers if we promise not to tell," Crystal says mischievously, leaning forward a bit to see

→ that hurt player, standing with help, coated in mud.

The crowd screams like it hasn't been screaming before and we give them their celebration—they deserve it, deserve for at least one teen to stand back up this month—then go wider, hover on the scoreboard.

It's halfway through the second quarter, zero to blinking zero, and all around the perimeter of the fence, spaced evenly, their hats in those clear plastic bags, are Dante's officers, gripping their shotguns, and, closer, closer, there's Dante, at the left edge of the stands, nearest the field. And he's hardly smiling, is rolling his toothpick in his mouth, is

→ now at a different, black and white angle. In a set of ghostly crosshairs, the rain all frozen around him.

Snap.

Dante's strobed silver, looks over to Jamie.

"Jackie Blue," Dante says.

"Jamie Lee," Jamie says back, not really grinning.

"Seriously?"

"Seriously."

"We need to talk."

"Sure," Jamie says, lowering his camera. "Can I just—?"

"You were the last one seen with her. And we haven't been able to find you all day."

"Deadline. Last night was big news. Midnight oil went all the way to that five o'clock whistle."

Dante smiles, takes Jamie by the scruff of his shirt, slams him closer all at once.

"Should have asked me who," Dante growls. "*Who* was the last one you were seen with. Isn't that your first W? 'Who, what, where, when, why?'"

"You're right," Jamie says, looking out at the game, Dante's hand just on his shoulder now. "I'm the reporter. You're the small town law enforcement. I guess when I write this up, I can characterize you *which*ever way I think best, yeah?

"Characterize this," Dante says, throwing Jamie forward, into the muck.

Jamie splats to the ground, his camera cracking open in some bad way.

"Don't get up," Dante tells him, and says into his shoulder mike that he's got a person here of not much interest, really, but let's confine him anyway. "Oh, and yeah," Dante adds. "He's kind of a clumsy one."

"Clumsy, gotcha," a woman's voice comes back.

"You can't, you can't," Jamie says, wiping his mouth, *not* standing, scrabbling for his camera, and we can tell by his eyes that he's not speaking to Dante but *for*

→ the people at the rails behind Dante, watching this. Waiting.

Dante doesn't even consider turning around, just removes his toothpick for once, talks loud enough that they can all hear: "In spite of my best efforts, a lot of these people have lost their sons and daughters this last week. They've lost friends and family. And right now I'm the only one standing between them and you, son. I don't know for sure if you're involved or not, but right now you're the best I got. And that might be good enough for tonight. In *this* small town, anyway."

The people behind Dante slash their eyes down at Jamie and walk on, ferrying their nachos and cokes up the aluminum steps, into the heavier and heavier rain.

Dante nods, looks away when the woman deputy hauls Jamie up roughly, taking extra care to accidentally grind his camera into more pieces than it already is.

"This is brutality," Jamie voices-over.

Dante smiles, watching the game again, his toothpick back in its place, his POV tracking a ball spiraling downfield, a Hail Mary if there ever was one, the Bulldog receiver rising up to meet it, catching it in the chest with both hands and splashing down hard on his back, at the Titan twenty.

Dante chocks his shotgun under his arm, claps loudly, and

→ the visiting head coach looks up to the Titan stands, cheering this Bulldog play on, and he nods to himself, spits, reseats his wet hat and turns back to the game.

Lindsay's standing at the metal door that will let them out of the booth for halftime, her dress shrouded under a football-player-sized Titans rain jacket.

Izzy and Crystal are covered up as well, though something about Izzy's hair is different.

Lindsay's studying her make-up in the mirrored back of the small square window, but now her POV's mostly on Crystal, just sitting there.

"What was it like?" Lindsay says back to her.

Crystal turns up to Lindsay, then comes down to Izzy, says, "What do you know?"

Izzy swallows.

"What was in the papers," Lindsay says for her. "Some freak with a bag over his head and a machete in his hand, a to-do list about eight kids long."

"Nine, counting me," Crystal says. "He was my big sister's ex. Kept trying to pop in, play like he was swimming in the victim pool too, but then sneak out, do his thing. Wasn't that hard to figure out."

"If you're watching on a screen it's not," Izzy chimes in. "If you're just in one room of a house, though, you don't know who's who in America, right?"

"I was just collateral damage," Crystal goes on. "I figured it out all by myself, but they'd left me behind, because I wasn't old enough. So I snuck out, found them, but then Rex—he was this other perv—he thought somebody was coming, and didn't want me to get caught out yet, so we fake kissed in the hay, so whoever it was would just keep walking. Except, well."

"It wasn't just anybody else," Lindsay finishes.

"And his hands up my shirt weren't all that fake," Crystal shrugs. "I guess I looked enough like her, though. To the first perv, I mean. Not the second."

"Bag Head," Izzy fills in.

"I shouldn't be here, either," Crystal says, and parts the front of her rain coat, scooches her short dress up past her boy shorts to show her stomach. Her no-joke scar.

"He liked to heat his machete up first," she says, smoothing her dress back down over her thighs.

"It made the wounds cauterize, not bleed out as fast. Saved my life and ruined it all at once. Doctor says if I ever get pregnant, that skin there might split, go all spontaneous cesarean, all chest-bursty. Pretty great, yeah?" Then, to Izzy: "Still wish it was you, brave girl?"

"I'm so sorry," Lindsay says.

"Long ago and far away," Crystal says, shrugging it off. "To keep any aliens from spurting up from my stomach, though, I get all the birth control I can handle, anyway. That allows certain . . . freedoms. So long as I don't ever decide to grow up, things are going to be pretty fine."

"Did she kill him?" Izzy says.

"My sister?"

Izzy considers her words, says, "If you were a surrogate for her, for him, then—"

"—your sister was the natural final girl," Lindsay finishes, asking the question as well.

Crystal studies

→ the field, a Titan runningback breaking free of the line,

running hard for maybe ten yards before the horde closes in on him, swallows him to the ground, yellow flags arcing through the air like dead canaries in the rain.

"*I* didn't get to," Crystal says, looking up to Izzy, then Lindsay.

"But you weren't—" Lindsay says.

"He should have killed me then," Crystal says. "I wanted that gas can, that match, that righteous kill. Now I'm in the sequel but never had the right kind of closure."

"You lived," Izzy says.

"He killed the good part of me," Crystal says. "Took it with him to hell."

Lindsay's just staring at Crystal.

Izzy scooches her hand over, to touch Crystal's, but Crystal looks down to this laughable effort, just smiles.

"Not to speak too ill of the dead either," Crystal says, turned away from Lindsay for this, "but there's a reason your boyfriend wasn't much use last weekend. Against Billie Jean, I mean."

"*What?*" Lindsay says, her fingertips to the hollow of her chest.

"Crystal, no," Izzy hisses.

Crystal's just smiling into her drop-dead beautiful reflection, though.

"It's because virgins are the only ones who are any good against a real slasher," Crystal voices-over, her grin in that glass sharp and mean.

"But—but we'd been together since seventh grade!" Lindsay says. "You didn't, you didn't move here until *ninth*."

Crystal shrugs, the answer too obvious to say.

"Bitch," Izzy says, staring out the glass now too.

"Survivor," Crystal corrects, and then the walkie-talkie on the counter before them crackles alive.

"Girls, girls!" Mrs. Graves is saying, so that Izzy leans forward, for an angle on Mrs. Graves, standing by the Cadillac, the roof ratcheting back.

"I think the rain's going to stop for us!" she screams over the roar of the crowd, and

→ yep: the drops are more scattered now, umbrellas folding in the stands, the scoreboard under two minutes now, and counting down.

"Well," Lindsay says, her eyes wet, lips tense.
Crystal stands, faces her.
"You look good," she says to Lindsay. "You'll win for sure."
Lindsay's just staring heat at her.
"We *all* grow suicidally beautiful at the beginning of October," she quotes back at Crystal.
Crystal smiles a bring-it-on smile and follows Lindsay out the door, leaving Izzy for one last look out at the serene football field, long enough to say, "*Suicidal*, anyway," and then

→ they're under the stands, still in their bulky raincoats, walking along a concrete path, their heads ducked like it's a Mean Joe Green tunnel they're passing through, from darkness to light, Dante the guard at the end of that tunnel, his back to them, his face dipped down to his shoulder mike.

"She's *what?*" he's saying into it, turning, seeing these three slow-motion girls approaching, his eyes about as close to what would have to be panic, on him.

"Stay here," he says to them, holding Lindsay by the shoulders to make this stick, then speaking into his mike: "Rodge, you and Cliff, under the stands, now. I want you to *personally* carry these three girls to my car, you got that? Rodge?"

Dante starts to walk away, comes back to the girls.

"My officers are on the way, you just need to stand right here, and don't let anybody approach, got it? Scream if they do, okay? And don't stop screaming."

"Th-thank you," Lindsay says for all three, and then Dante's running, Lindsay's face instantly shifting back to magazine-cover mode.

"Everybody wants to ruin our special day, don't they?" she says to Crystal and Izzy, and, of the three of them, Izzy's the only one to stop, track Dante for a few steps, as if she can tunnel ahead

→ to where he's going: the skewed, shaky image of that woman deputy, butterflied open in the backseat of her cruiser but still alive somehow, the blue and red lights above her slowly rolling, her eyes open, staring above, through the headliner, at

→ a football hanging forever in the misty air like it's that same punt from hours before.

It tumbles through the darkness and leftover rain, through the stadium lights, and, miles below it the clock on the scoreboard zeroes out, the buzzer going off, the audience standing to cheer,

→ the marching band slopping through the muck, their sound covering

→ the Cadillac's ignition turning over, the hand guiding it Mrs. Graves'.

Principal Masters steps out onto the red-clay track, the thoroughly streamered homecoming baton in one hand, a bullhorn in his other, some kind of announcements and thanks to the visiting team happening but they're lost, now look to be introductions for the homecoming candidates this year, and, under the stands,

→ it's what we've all been waiting for: still walking in slow motion, Lindsay and Crystal and Izzy cross some magical barrier between the real world and the timeless land of glamour shots:

→ Lindsay trailing her coat off her shoulders elegantly, her dress red-carpet worthy times two, and slinky, cut to fit, to allow for her sling, even, and the train—*train?*—it's trailing behind her but somehow never quite touching the ground, her good shoulder bare and tanned, a swirl of cut-outs in her dress snaking fingerwide ripples of flesh down along her side to her leg, her chin set in satisfaction;

→ Crystal letting her jacket go behind her, stepping out of it so that all there is at first is bare leg and impossibly high heel, next her short cocktail kind of dress, very classy, very proper, very surprising for her even if it's not a proper homecoming dress, and this isn't a Megan Fox under-the-hood moment, and it isn't Shannon Elizabeth through a hidden camera, this is Sheena Easton strutting out in front of everybody, her eyes dialed up to Susanna Hoffs, this is Ursula Andress, rising from that blue surf. This is Crystal Blake, saying under her breath, "What would you little maniacs like to do first?"

Just in case we can't tell she's upstaging Lindsay, either, we look

→ ahead, for Lindsay's tight-lipped reaction to the crowd's swelling noise;

→ to Mrs. Graves covering her mouth with her hand;

→ to Principal Masters, suddenly wordless, his bullhorn squealing;

→ to an unclaimed, breathing POV watching from under the stands;

→ but then we have to dive back immediately for Izzy, trying to untangle herself from her rain jacket, having to stumble ahead out of it, shake it off behind her.

Her dress, though—*now* we can see what's different about her hair.

She's dyed her streaks to match the demure pink skull bleeding down the side of this scaly grey armless take on a kimono, but the real attention keeper is the police tape she's got draped across her like a beauty pageant sash, like the skull's peeking out from under that do-not-cross line.

And of course no heels like Lindsay and Crystal, just her same clunky combat boots, only with fat pink laces for tonight, and, on her shoulder, a sparkly letter *B* brooch she's touching for strength, her lips tight, her steps nervous, her POV turning scarily up to this wall of people watching her. This wall of people not clapping, just trying to figure out exactly what she's wearing, here, and whether it's an insult or not—whether she's making a mockery of the dead or claiming some kinship. The band starts in to fill the empty space and Izzy turns her eyes forcefully away from them, to Crystal's ass in front of her, a re-do of the opening scene of Bogey's party, pretty much. Which is our cue to cut to

→ the three of them already standing on the trunk and backseat of the Cadillac, Mrs. Graves behind the wheel.

"Your mother let you wear that?" Lindsay hisses through her smile to Izzy.

"Your mother let you live?" Crystal says back to Lindsay, not even having to look over to deliver it.

"Actually, she's probably having a cute little heart attack right about—" Izzy says, and like that we're

→ back in her POV, scanning hard for her mom, her dad.

Nowhere.

Nowhere nowhere nowhere.

Principal Masters steps up onto the bumper then, his weight making the whole car sink a little.

"Everybody do whatever the opposite of a rain dance is!" he says, smiling, waiting for everybody to laugh with him.

Crickets.

He takes it in stride, switches the bullhorn to his good hand.

"And now their daaaaaaates!" he announces, trilling it out wrestling style, holding the homecoming baton high.

Izzy's reaction is pure terror.

Walking out of a GQ ad to take Crystal's hand is the Ponyboy she was talking to at Bogey's party. His tux is grey and pinstriped, the collar loose, bowtie already hanging like it's the afterparty.

He takes her hand, turns around for the crowd so she can stand there with her hands on his shoulders, the flashes popping.

Then, from the other side of the stands, a string of firecrackers go off and a roman candle lobs its flare up into the air over the field.

Women in the stands scream, people mutter, Masters lowers his bullhorn uncertainly, and Titan comes out on the shoulders of the Bulldog cheerleaders.

The crowd goes even insaner than it was for Crystal.

"Who?" Izzy says, but then Titan's kneeling, two of the Bulldog cheerleaders lifting his head off.

Inside, it's a mummy, it's the English patient, it's

→ "Jake," Izzy says, close up. Painfully.

He stands, his cartoon mitts taking Lindsay by the waist, twirling her out and around then setting her back where she was like she weighs nothing.

"Do mascots have, you know, proper equipment?" Crystal says out loud, smiling. Lindsay cuts her eyes across at her but is already reaching back into the Cadillac, down alongside the closed passenger door, between it and the white leather seat, coming up with the sword, polished to a chrome blindness.

She holds it up while everyone cheers, and a gust of rain sweeps across the car, threatening to fold the roof up.

Lindsay Skywalkers the sword higher into the sky, for the crowd, the water beading down it, and her, and all of them.

"Dante okayed this?" Izzy says back to Mrs. Graves, but Mrs. Graves is crying from the power of the moment, trying to wipe away the tears.

Izzy leans back up into her place in this line-up, still politely clapping, Titan taking the sword now, touching its tip to the ground and kneeling behind it, saying to the audience no, no, *you*.

Masters sets the bullhorn down to lead this round of clapping, Izzy's POV desperately searching the stands, the faces, the wings, the field, for

→ "Dad?" she's saying. "Mom?"

Nowhere.

Her breathing is getting heavier now, her eyes worried, about to spill over, and now Masters has the bullhorn again, is clicking it open.

"And last but certainly not least," he says, "and probably in a matching ensemble . . . "

He turns with flourish to the ramp Ponyboy walked up.

The crowd stands, starts clapping, but there's no one.

The applause dies off.

"No," Izzy says, a tear actually feeling down her face now, Lindsay and Crystal looking over to her in anticipation if not sympathy, Masters tongue-tied, trying to come up with something.

"Not now, you prick, not this time, not again," Izzy's saying, and just as she's turning away from the crowd to hide for the rest of her life, a flutter of motion catches her eye.

And everybody else's.

There's no jumbotron, but there ought to be.

It's Ben, cleaned up and in a poorly fitting suit, his hair plastered to his head, his tie perfect.

He's walking up that ramp, staring so hard at Izzy.

She smiles, holds her hand out, the crowd clapping for him but not yelling this time, and when Ben gets there Izzy lowers her face enough to ask, careful not to show anything to the crowd, "Where are they?"

Ben shrugs a knowing shrug, sending us

→ all the way across Rivershead for the explanation.

To Izzy's house.

To the driveway, both these expensive cars cocked at wrong angles in the driveway, Jigsaw-brand metal cages booted around each of their outside rear tires, big enough that the metal's chewed up into the fender, is permanently snarled in place, Izzy's dad sitting on the border of a flowerbed in his rumpled suit, a half-emptied bottle in his hand, Izzy's mom walking up the driveway, looking out into the road.

This is what Ben was making in the basement last night, yes. His

→ smile tells us so, and, backing off a bit, Izzy's hands are gripping his shoulders in thanks.

Crystal reaches a hand over, places it on top of one of Izzy's.

Izzy's just staring out at all this proudly, her face still wet,

→ Mrs. Graves completing that motion for her, lowering a tissue from her face, her wrist catching the Cadillac's shifter, jerking the whole party forward a foot or two.

Nobody falls but everybody's different, kind of smiling their questions back to Mrs. Graves, who has her shoulders raised in comical apology.

"Not yet!" Lindsay hisses back to Mrs. Graves, and something about this makes Izzy turn around. Not to Mrs. Graves but the opposite direction, the far side of the stands.

What she's seeing, what she can't even find the right profanity for,

→ it's Wildfire, blind and bandaged, being led out onto the track by a football player in full, muddy pads.

Various women in the crowd stand, crying softly, and, on cue, the speakers start into *she ran calling Wi-ildfire*, and then everybody's swaying with it, a lighter or two flaring on against the drizzle.

Lindsay stands, her hands balled together under her chin in teary-eyed surprise, and, when she reaches across to the not-there-yet Wildfire, Jake lifts her by the waist again, sets her sidesaddle on the horse's back.

She leans forward to hug Wildfire, draping herself along him like a mermaid would have to, her good arm to the crowd, up along Wildfire's neck, her hand scrunching up into his mane, her eyes closed in what can only be interpreted as true love.

"Everybody loves a good donkey show," Crystal says, just loud enough, her face pleasant for the crowd.

"She kept it *alive?*" Izzy says, in complete wonder, and already Jake-as-Titan is leading Wildfire by the bridle, back behind the car.

"The stupid leading the blind," Crystal says through her smile, and Jake flashes his mummy eyes up at her but—

"Now for the victory lap before the queen is crowned!" Masters is already saying through the bullhorn, Wildfire mostly in place behind the car, Lindsay's

→ POV chancing down onto that shiny rear bumper.

A distinct pair of brown and white cowboy boots there, toes up.

She screams, Wildfire prancing back, flaring his nostrils, and Jake reels him down, helps Lindsay stay on in her slick dress, finally looks down to what everybody's seeing now: two cowboy boots we know and dread, toes up. Only there because Mrs. Graves burped the Cadillac forward.

"Not karma not karma not karma," Izzy's saying, stepping down, and when she sees the boots, so definitely Brittney's, she opens her mouth to scream, can't even do that.

"Uh-oh," Crystal says, beside Izzy now, then, calling over the Cadillac to Mrs. Graves. "I think you hit something, Mrs. Graves."

Mrs. Graves stands away from her seat to try to see,

→ her right foot slipping into the gas pedal,

→ the Cadillac surging forward again, off Brittney, who drags with it a foot or two, her hands tied above her head with a thick rope, the rope apparently tied to the frame of the Cadillac.

Izzy collapses over her as if protecting her, her hands furious on the knot but Brittney's wrapped in iridescent videotape that's confusing everything.

"You were right, it was, it was—" Brittney says up into Izzy's ear.

"Somebody cut this!" Izzy screams up to the world, and

→ we go close on Jake's eyes, gears clanking in there.

He steps in with the sword.

"Look out," he says, and brings the sword down, cleanly severing the rope, Brittney pulling her hands to her chest, smiling, Izzy hugging her.

"My fault, my fault," Izzy's saying to Brittney, pulling her close, saying right into her ear, "my fault, I killed the sheriff."

Brittney pushes her back a bit, looks up to her with wonder.

"Then—then it's you," she says. "You're the final girl."

"No, it was an accident, it was stupid, I'm not—"

"You look so beautiful," Brittney says up to Izzy, even reaching up to touch the sparkly *B* Izzy's wearing, and spills more tears. Izzy runs Brittney's still-dry bangs from her face.

They blow right back.

The Cadillac's thick exhaust is right on top of them.

"Eww, 1972," Jake says, and looks up to Mrs. Graves, waves her forward with the sword, and Mrs. Graves complies, her

→ POV looking very intentionally down to the pedals now.

She punches the right one about forty-two times too hard—either that or that 500 under the hood's more than she expects. Either way

→ the Cadillac spins its tires against the clay, pulling forward again,

→ hard enough for a razor-thin black cable wrapped around Brittney's neck to snap tight,

→ hard enough for the cable looped around her boots to become obvious, the stakes holding it down to the track obvious, the chalk it's buried under obvious, *every*thing obvious,

→ except it's all too late: Brittney's head pops cleanly off, her torso jerking up, pumping blood from its neck stump, her head doing that *Prom Night* roll across the red clay, taking its place in the line of memorial photos.

Izzy screams, pulling Brittney close, her dress slathered in hot blood and gore, and

→ in the Cadillac, Mrs. Graves screams, the Cadillac fishtailing ahead dangerously, a *different* line snapping up from under a white line of chalk, now, also tied to the frame of the car. We follow the cable as it pulls tight, we barrel down the guitar string it is now until we see it's tied to the main electrical junction for the stadium, back at the field house.

And then that giant breaker box jerks off the wall in a cascade of sparks.

In the parking lot, standing by the woman deputy's cruiser, Dante looks over to the stadium, says it for us: "Oh shit."

The stadium lights are all dying as one, the clouds opening up in a peal of thunder, a sheet of rain coming down on the field like judgment.

The crowd, already in a panic, scatters more, some of them jumping off the side of the stands from too high, others spilling down the stairs, a few crashing the announcer's box, fighting to pack themselves in.

Mrs. Graves abandons the Cadillac, leaving it in gear so it noses into the fence just down from the stands, pushes it in a bit, its exhaust coughing once, going quiet for the entrance of what we've all been secretly waiting for: standing at the fifty-yard line, outlined in a nimbus of rain, it's Billie Jean, that long black sword hanging down from his hand.

"So this is how it is, then," Jake says up to Lindsay, about the

Billie Jean they can both see.

"*What?*" she shrieks back to him with her whole body.

Jake just shakes his head, plants the *real* sword ahead of him in the field and steps out of his Titan gear.

Underneath, it's a zip-up hoodie, jeans, sneakers.

He looks out to Billie Jean, approaching at his fast-slow slasher pace, starts unwinding the bandages from his face so we finally get to see his wounds, running with rain.

It's not Red Skull. More like Two-Face, especially when he smiles.

"Looks like I'm going to have to save the day again," he says, and walks past the sword, picking it up on the way like a hero, Izzy's

→ POV just seeing him walk off, then reaching down for the thin cable that so ingeniously decapitated Brittney.

It doesn't make sense.

Out on the field now, closer to the home side of the track than not, the two swords clash together, clash together again, even sparking a bit.

Behind them, Wildfire rears up, slashing the air dramatically with his hooves, Lindsay barely clinging to him.

The swords come together again, and Jake's faster than Billie Jean, is having fun with this, is playing *Kill Bill* to Billie Jean's Drago while:

→ Dante's pushing through the gate by the ticket booth, spitting his toothpick out on the way, a serious rifle cocked up on his shoulder, murder in his eyes;

→ Izzy's trying to pull Brittney back to the fence for some reason but Brittney's feet are still staked down, Izzy pulling anyway, still trying to save her;

→ Lindsay's wheeling on Wildfire, Wildfire screaming, blind, blood frothing at his nostrils;

→ Crystal's standing just off the side of the stands, watching this develop, a memory sparking in her eyes;

→ Ben's sliding out into the muck to pull Izzy away from Brittney's body, Izzy fighting him, lost in some panic attack, refusing to accept that this is all happening,

→ but it is.

Out on the field, Jake finally gets too fancy with his samurai posturing. Billie Jean clatters his fancy sword away.

Jake just smiles, drops to his knees, parts his hoodie at the chest, daring Billie Jean to run him through.

Billie Jean cocks his head, doesn't seem to understand but does it anyway: steps forward, thrusting the sword into Jake's chest.

But not.

The sword doesn't go in.

Jake smiles, knocks on his chest with his knuckles, showing off the vest.

"If it was good enough for April Ripley's stupid little pop gun, it's good enough for you," he says.

At which point Billie Jean unsheathes a machete from his overalls, says in Jamie's voice, "How high's that vest go?" and slices the machete around sideways, lopping Jake's head off so easily.

For a few long moments in the rain, Jake stays there on his knees, his trachea white, somehow longer than his neck stump, like a worm trying to crawl out.

Then Billie Jean walks past, his eyeholed POV fixed on Izzy, Ben fully aware of Billie Jean, trying to pull her away even more desperately.

But it's so slick, they can't get purchase, and everything's going quiet now, quiet enough for

→ Izzy to look up, her face serene, and say, "This *is* that kind of movie."

Which makes her stand, holding onto Ben.

Together they climb over the bottom rail of the stands just as

→ Dante's barreling up the ramp, about to burst out, so intent on the approaching Billie Jean that he never sees Crystal, reaching through the rails to trip him with the homecoming baton.

He spills hard, his head slamming into a bench, knocking him useless, the gun clattering ahead of him.

Crystal walks ahead to it, pulls it cleanly through, says back to him, "I've got this, Deputy,"

→ and now Billie Jean's clambering easily over the rail after Izzy and Ben, Izzy falling backwards and up, her POV looking ahead, where they're going: to the top rail.

A dead end. A fast drop. Just like the cliff.

"Stupid girls run upstairs, stupid girls run upstairs," she's saying to herself, turning to pull Ben with her up the aluminum steps, Billie Jean just feet behind them,

→ Crystal down on the track, Billie Jean in the crosshairs of Dante's rifle, about to have his insides opened up.

"Now, you fucker," Crystal says, and pulls the trigger.

On nothing.

She doesn't understand this gun.

She drops it to her chest, clicking everything, pulling the trigger: nothing.

She looks to Dante for help, and when he's still not moving, her POV looks up to

→ what we're already on: Ben, pushing Izzy ahead of him, hard enough that she can't be the big sister, hard enough that she can just keep falling up, falling up.

Then Billie Jean hooks a finger into Ben's suit jacket.

Ben slithers out, spills ahead, but they're almost to the top rail now, too.

This can't go on.

He looks up to Izzy one last time then turns around, sets his feet on the stairs. He bends down between the seats and comes up with a red and gold golf umbrella somebody left open, rolling in the wind.

He snicks it shut, holds it by the J-handle, slashes it back and forth in the air between him and Billie Jean.

"Stay the fuck away from my sister, you son of a bitch," he says, tapping the tip of the sword on the stair between him and Billie Jean, and Billie Jean shakes his head at how stupid this is, but is raising the sword anyway, to do what has to be done, Izzy screaming no, fighting back to get between Ben and Billie Jean but she's not going to make it she's not going to make—

And then we're in the least likely spot, suddenly: tight on the back of Crystal's spike heels.

Because her dress is puddling down around them.

We back up and she's in her boy shorts and strapless bra, just standing there in the rain.

"*Hey!*" she says up to Billie Jean, her voice cutting through the heart of the night. "This is what you want, isn't it?" and then reaches back with one hand, undoes her bra

→ Ben definitely frozen in those headlights

→ but of course we're over her shoulder here, can't quite see all of what she's showing, even though we wheel around for her wicked grin when she says to Billie Jean that "They're real, and they're spectacular,"

→ and Billie Jean, he's already turned from Ben's *completely* slack face to Crystal, and—he is a slasher after all—he's caught in amber, he's walking through honey, he's twelve-years-old again, can't even hope to tear his eyes away, his sword twitching in his hand, and the moment's dilated enough for each raindrop to have definition, the world's suddenly turning slow enough that

→ Dante's service revolver can stab a finger of flame out over the top of an aluminum bench, *blast* the night even more open

→ Billie Jean aware of that flash in the same moment that slug's barreling through time and space for him

→ Dante saying it once and for all, his chin resting on the bench: "Smile, you fucker," his shot

→ dead-on, spattering Izzy and Ben with Billie Jean's blood, Izzy's POV looking up to Billie Jean wavering there, blood spilling from under his mask.

He falls, his foot catching on a bench so he doesn't roll down, Dante standing groggy from where he fell, trying to clear his own blood from his eyes so he can fire again if he needs to.

Izzy steps forward gingerly, her palm in Ben's chest to keep him back.

"Is it, is it over?" Ben asks, a kid now, again. Like he should be.

He looks past Billie Jean to Crystal, shimmying back into her wet dress.

Izzy doesn't answer him, her eyes intent on this Billie Jean.

She lowers herself to him slowly.

"Hey, horror girl," Crystal calls out from the track, tucking her breasts back in, our *and* Ben's POV a breath too late for that.

Izzy looks down to her.

"You of anybody should know they always come back up," Crystal says, about Billie Jean.

"That's just in the movies," Izzy says, and pulls the mask off Jamie's head, uncatches his leg from the bench, sending him tumbling down the stands, spilling through the rails, splashing into the mud at Crystal's feet.

Slowly and intentionally, and with relish, Crystal inserts her heel into Jamie's eye anyway, and pushes in, her POV enjoying every inch of that gory close-up, finishing her story out at last, cutting us ahead to

→ the parking lot of the high school, thick with sirens again, Dante sitting in the back of an ambulance getting the bandage-headband treatment;

→ Crystal the absolute darling of every camera out there, the homecoming baton casual in her hand like it doesn't even matter;

→ Lindsay out on the field, mostly alone, walking Wildfire back and forth, trying to calm him.

Behind her, sitting on the trunk of the Cadillac, Izzy is staring into the glow of her phone, at

→ a photo of Brittney. But then the phone rings in her hand. The display reads "DAD."

Izzy pulls the phone to her ear, says, "Dad?"

Beat, beat.

"I saw the, the news," he says.

"Yeah," Izzy says, "it was—"

"Just wanted to see if you were all right," he says, and Izzy has to pull her wet eyes away, out to Lindsay, with Wildfire,

→ but it's evidently too dark for her to see the Titan sword lying in the wet grass, a little evidence flag numbering it off.

Or: why be trying to look at it, right?

It's a nice final image, anyway, and Izzy's story feels done now, except, even closer on that sword, on the handle, a crusty hand is picking it up.

It takes us out on the field with Lindsay. She's leading Wildfire by the bridle, whispering to him, her face tear-streaked one more time, but she's not out in the parking lot soaking up the attention, either.

Her story's winding down, too.

To prove it, the next time she looks up, the real Billie Jean is standing there in the light rain just ahead of her, the bright sword angling down from his hand, his white leg brace practically glowing in the dark.

Wildfire's nostrils flare and he screams, rising up onto his back legs.

Lindsay falls away,

→ Izzy looking up to this commotion, then to the track, the stands, for anybody.

They're alone out here.

She stands to see better,

→ but can't hear Lindsay saying "No, no," falling backwards into the muddy field.

Billie Jean walks steadily towards her out of the drizzle, is almost there when Wildfire skitters away, Lindsay still holding his bridle.

It swings her around, and for a second we're sure she's going under those stomping hooves, but then—this isn't her first rodeo.

She slithers up onto the back somehow, her dress hiked way up so she can sit right.

"*You're dead!*" she screams down at Billie Jean.

That doesn't stop him walking towards her.

"No," Izzy says, stepping down off the Cadillac, walking through the muck the track is now, so she's standing in front of the stands, near where Jamie fell through.

In her POV, Billie Jean's . . . reaching for Wildfire's bridle?

"Brooks Baker," Izzy says, impressed.

Wildfire tears away just like he must have before, though, rises on his haunches, slashing the air, one of those massive hooves connecting, dropping Billie Jean to the ground like a bowling ball.

Wildfire prances away, Lindsay working his reins, her eyes hot on Billie Jean, who, who's

→ the close up of his right hand, it still has the hilt of that sword, and the sword's upright.

He slams the butt of the sword into the ground in anger, splashing, and what we think at first is that he's planting it there, that this is going to be the pike that drives up into Wildfire's chest, but

→ then he's standing again. Breathing hard.

"*Nooooo!*" Lindsay screams down at him, and charges Wildfire into him, over him, and then comes back across him *again*, bouncing as hard as she can on the saddle to push Wildfire's hooves even deeper,

→ Dante standing from the ambulance in the parking lot, narrowing his eyes at the back of the stands. At the field.

"Cop radar?" the woman paramedic says, maybe tending him overmuch, here.

"Shhh," he says, angling his head over to listen

"Stay down, stay down," Izzy's saying, too terrified to step out onto the playing field.

But Billie Jean, who it would seem has to be dead here, he isn't.

He stands again, slashing the air with his sword.

One of those cuts nicks Wildfire again, and Wildfire screams, rears back, almost spilling Lindsay.

She loses the reins, clamps onto the saddle horn, and Wildfire's in a panic now, remembers this sword, these cuts.

He wheels around, slams his hooves into the mud and's already streaking off to the left, Lindsay bouncing, just trying to hold on, the stirrups flapping.

Billie Jean lumbers off that same direction.

The night swallows them.

Dante rounds the corner, his pistol already out, his head bandaged, eyes intense.

Izzy's just standing there, nearly hyperventilating.

Dante takes her by the shoulders, shakes her.

"What the hell happened?" he bellows down to her.

Izzy pushes away, falls to her knees, turns to the side to throw up.

Dante spins away, giving her space, and Izzy makes use of it: in the mud and vomit, her hand's finding something.

A cell phone?

She palms it, climbs the fence back up.

"Her dad?" Dante says, walking in a circle practically but trying to contain his anger here. Trying not to yell at Izzy, anyway.

Izzy nods once, yes.

Dante spins away, holding the handle of his revolver to his bandaged forehead.

Izzy's just staring out at the field, now.

"Where—did you see where they were going?" Dante says then. "Which direction?"

Izzy swallows, looks in all the directions available to her.

"Does she have her phone with her?" Dante says then, looking down to the one in Izzy's hand.

Izzy looks down to it as well, breathes, looks back up to Dante and pulls her own out, its display so obviously cracked, the screen flickering like always.

"Mine—mine broke," she says, then holds up the other phone: "I was, she was letting me use hers to call my dad."

Not the answer Dante was looking for.

The rest of his troops round the corner then, and more besides. State police, it looks like. Firemen. Paramedics. The pitchfork and torch crowd, finally assembled.

"Where is she?" a woman yells, and she looks so much like Lindsay that she has to be her mom.

Somebody tries to calm her.

"Stratford?" Dante says to Izzy, his voice all the way in control now.

Izzy breathes, looking around to everybody, to the phone in her hand, and then she nods to herself, some decision made.

"You know how these kind of movies work," she says to Dante. "They always go back to the scene of the crime, to end where they started. Mr. Pleasance, he, he says it's structural, that it creates a circle, that—"

"*Where*," Dante says.

"The river," Izzy says, looking to her right, where it must be. "The cliff."

Dante studies her, considering this, then turns, says it loud enough for all of Rivershead to hear: "Lookout Point, they're going out to the point!"

Feet splash, motors start, a helicopter thumps alive and Izzy's just standing there alone, her breath still hitching.

Dante comes back to her, says, "You say you were calling your dad?"

"He'll be here in two minutes," Izzy recites, holding the phone up as some kind of proof.

"Straight home, now," Dante says to her, and Izzy nods that she knows, she knows, then Dante turns, is gone.

Izzy just stands there in the rain, hugging herself.

Finally she looks left, where Lindsay and Billie Jean *really* went, and it's all about her eyes. What she thinks. What she knows.

A half-breath later that showboat of a Cadillac is pulling up to a large dark house, a monstrous dark barn, the one we know from Lindsay's famous ride. The Cadillac's headlights are harsh yellow, then clicking off.

Sitting behind the wheel, the top down above her, is Izzy, soaking wet.

She steps up over the side and her combat boots splash down into the mud.

She pushes the side door of the barn open, lights her Zippo.

Standing there in the open space between the stalls is Wildfire, slathered in sweat, Lindsay exhausted on his back, looking up at Izzy through wet bangs.

"He here yet?" Izzy says.

"How'd you know?" Lindsay says back.

"'A good horse will always go back to the barn at the end of the day,'" Izzy quotes, looking past her flame at this cavernous barn.

Instead of just being a ground-level under a hay loft, it's got two levels above that, maybe, and some kind of chute-and-bucket shaft big enough for a car, going right up to the roof, a block and tackle system to feed it, ropes on pulleys trailing all down through it in the most complicated fashion.

There's hay and tack everywhere, horse eyes glittering from the double row of stalls.

"This a barn or a mall?" Izzy says.

"Careful with that," Lindsay says, about Izzy's Zippo, and Izzy cuts her eyes at Lindsay.

"What are you saying?" she asks.

"Just that this is a barn full of hay and animals. Nothing about janitors, okay?"

"That wasn't me."

Lindsay shrugs, not pushing it. Not *needing* to push it.

Izzy follows her light to

→ a bank of light switches. She hits a few at random, lights the place up unevenly, pockets her lighter.

"So this is it, then?" she says, panning around. "The big final stand."

"To be honest," Lindsay says, sliding off Wildfire's back. "I thought it would be at the dance."

"Where everybody could see?"

Lindsay doesn't dignify this.

"Aren't you supposed to shoot them when they're like that?" Izzy says, about Wildfire.

"Do you know horses or do you watch westerns?"

"You saying there's a difference?"

"I love him. He saved my life."

Izzy doesn't pursue this.

"He'll just be expecting *you*," she says. "Not me. That's our advantage."

"You think he actually . . . 'expects' anymore?"

"You're the one with the connections," Izzy says. "What do you call him, Billie Jean or Daddy?"

"Fuck you."

"Eww, profanity. I wouldn't even be involved if you hadn't roped me in, you know?"

"And I wouldn't have even asked you to participate if your mother hadn't politely *suggested* it," Lindsay says back.

Izzy shakes her head. Turns her POV away, her hand pulling on one of the ropes in the silo of a chute. It's on some counterweight, its large hook coming up a foot or two.

"*Blair Witch*," she says, disgusted.

"What?"

"We're fighting with each other instead of, you know. Teaming up. Fighting him. That's how the horror always wins, yeah? Divide and conquer."

"I know. I've read your cute little papers, remember?"

Izzy just stares at her. "I'm here to help you, you know," she says.

"You're here for revenge."

"The Billie Jean who killed Brittney's already dead. I'm done, wash my hands and walk away."

"Can't let go, though, can you?" Lindsay says, smiling conspiratorially. "Want to see him in real life just one more time, right?"

"I told Dante and them to go back out to where it started."

"The Point."

Izzy nods.

"Good," Lindsay says, working her phone up from her bra, because homecoming dresses don't have pockets.

"Not *for* you, but because it has to *be* you," Izzy says. "If *they* pop him, he'll just keep coming back. You know this as well as I do. Don't lie."

Lindsay, unsaddling Wildfire, shrugs.

"I had mono in sixth grade," she says. "My brother brought me all his old movies. It was fun for a month, but, you know, I got better."

"I don't think so. You got infected."

"They're not movies," Lindsay says, more serious now, "they're survival guides. Do this, you live. Do that, you don't. How do you think I made it through last time? Luck? Pilates?"

"You stayed a virgin all this time just so you could be a final girl?"

Lindsay smiles, says, "Well, the movies didn't get every little part of the formula right."

"You're not even real, then. Not even a real final girl."

Lindsay turns on Izzy now. "There are no real final girls. Get that through your dyed hair if you can. That day is long over."

"That's what everybody still wants, though. All Golden Age, right?"

"So that's what you give them. Just never let them behind the curtain."

"Like I am now."

"And your word's so believable in this town. Sluts always want to bring the good girls down to their level."

"And so what if I am?"

"You've got a whole section of the video store to spread out in," Lindsay shrugs, hanging Wildfire's bridle on a brass hook. "Or sometimes it's a room, like. With a curtain for a door, right?"

"If I were going to do porn, I *would* be a star," Izzy says. "You got that right at least."

"'If,'" Lindsay says. "Good, pretend."

"I can't believe I used to want to be like you."

"You and the rest."

"I hope he kills you."

"Don't you worry about that. I've got something ready for him."

Izzy looks around, looks around, her POV cataloging the pitchforks, the pint-sized tractor, the display of hay hooks on one post.

"You thought it was going to be at the dance, though," she says.

"Final girls are like girl scouts," Lindsay says, pulling a long, thin cable down from a shelf. "We're always prepared. Now, help or go home, okay? It's do or die time, here. And you might just learn something."

When Izzy doesn't leave, Lindsay tosses a loop of cable across to her, leads her

→ to the row of stables.

They're immaculate, are maple or mahogany or something sweet and hardwood, kept at a deep luster, six to a side, just one stall empty.

The horses stamp and blow.

"We're not going to use the big obvious hook over there?" Izzy asks. "The tractor? All those blade things?"

"This your show or mine?" Lindsay says back, threading the hooped end of her side of the cable through a flange on the first stable's latch.

Izzy watches, doesn't get it.

"Just do the same over there," Lindsay says, "you'll see."

Izzy shakes her head but does it, until they meet at the other end.

"This is the genius part, now," Lindsay says, and crosses to some kind of rich-person farrier booth, almost like a shoe-shine station, just for horses.

Lindsay reaches into a bucket, comes out with a funny looking, flat-headed nail. Then another.

She tosses one to Izzy, takes her own to the hooped end of the cable and threads it through the hoop, pulling the cable tight behind it and not letting that tension off, or else the nail will fall, the cable slipping back through.

"Over there," Lindsay says, directing Izzy, and Izzy does the same on her side, walking the tension past each latch until her and Lindsay's hands meet where the cable does.

Lindsay steps her hand over Izzy's, has all the tension now but isn't pulling too hard.

"I always wanted to try both sides at once," she says. "Thanks. Now, that door you came in. Lock it. Except for the big doors, there's just the one from the back," she says, nodding through the stalls to the obvious door down at the end of their hall. "And that's the one he likes."

Izzy

→ goes back, sets the lock on the door she came in through.

Her eyes are wrong, though.

She's thinking too much, lost in something. She runs her palm along Wildfire's side then

→ ducks under the tight cables, steps out into the space between the stalls, her back to Lindsay, her jaw working in thought.

"You don't want to be there," Lindsay says. "Take Wildfire's stall, it's empty. Wait, no, I know. Get a little of that hay, put it on the floor there."

Izzy looks to the cement floor she's standing on.

"'Come with me if you want to live,'" Lindsay quotes, smiling, and Izzy

→ has done it, put a little armful of hay there in a tight pile.

"Now light it," Lindsay whispers. "Use your school spirit, girl. I know you've got it."

Izzy glares at Lindsay and stands to leave.

"You want him dead this time, don't you?" Lindsay says. "Isn't that why you're here?"

"I'm not burning your barn down. Like you said, who's going to believe me when I say you told me to?"

"It won't—" Lindsay smiles, still pulling back on the cables, "their feet will put it out, and there's just dirt where they're going anyway. It won't spread. Are you not AP *any*thing?"

"I don't know why—"

"You can't *handle* the truth," Lindsay says, laughing at herself, her references coming nervously fast now.

Izzy, still shaking her head, lights the small pyre, the

→ smoke drifting up, around.

The horses go freaking *insane*, kicking at the half doors of their stalls, screaming so that Izzy nearly falls down, away from it all.

"Go!" Lindsay tells her then, and Izzy stumbles over to the stall with the "Wildfire" plaque, crawls under the door into that musty darkness.

She stands, looks around, fingertips to the wall in honor, and says, as if just now figuring it out: "It ends where it started, right?"

Then she's looking over the top of the stall. At Lindsay, keeping that cable tight, not favoring her shoulder as much anymore. At the horse across from her, losing it completely, a demon on hooves.

Then down to the thin black cable running through the latch of that horse's half door.

Izzy chocks herself up on her armpits on top of her door, reaches down for the cable, to feel it again.

"This is—" she says, looking up to Lindsay with new eyes, and

→ again that cable snaps tight around Brittney's throat.

"This is," Izzy says again, but sees it in Lindsay's face: the back door, it's creaking open. She cranks her head over as best she can, peers her POV through the smoke, and, right on time, his entrance more grim than Crystal's at the game but still pretty grand, it's Brooks Baker, dead so many times it doesn't even matter any more.

The reason it doesn't matter is that he's Billie Jean, now.

He steps in, his sword held low, the horses crazy loud, smoke thick in the air.

"Daddy, I'm over here," Lindsay calls out in a little girl voice, and Billie Jean's face pops up.

He evaluates her, evaluates this, and starts his long, ponderous walk, the tip of that sword dragging the dirt, then the concrete, meaning

→ it's time.

Lindsay pulls back hard on her cable and all the latches pop at once, the doors swinging open as one, the horses exploding from their stalls, trampling the fire, pounding up the concrete to that back door they seem to know.

Right into Billie Jean, yes.

Lindsay steps up alongside Wildfire's swinging stall door, doesn't look in.

"And that's how a final girl does it," she says.

"This the version we'll see in the papers?" Izzy says, and Lindsay finally does give Izzy her attention, the dust and smoke still too heavy to make out Billie Jean's surely-shattered form anyway.

"What are you saying?"

"We only have your word about what went down two weekends ago," Izzy says, still speaking from the darkness.

"I told him—"

"Jamie Curtis, you mean? The wannabe Billie Jean? You told him the story the two of you came up with together, that about the shape of it?"

As punctuation, Izzy punches the cell phone in her hand alive.

It's the one she found in the mud.

Now Lindsay's POV can settle on Izzy's glowing face. Her knowing face.

"Did you think I wouldn't recognize it," she says, nodding down to the cable Lindsay still has looped in her hand.

"You just think you do."

"No," Izzy says punching her thumb into the phone, "I *know* I do."

An instant later, Lindsay's right breast glows green.

Her phone.

"Is his name really even Jamie Curtis?" Izzy says. "Or was that y'all's personal little joke?"

Lindsay shakes her head about all this. Studies the smoke and dust still hanging at the other end of the stalls. Finally decides: "Some people are born lucky," she says, gathering the cable in her hands while she speaks. "I found him when he wrote up Bag Head— Crystal's wannabe little episode? We found we . . . shared certain predilections, you could say. He's the real reason you got your homecoming bid, too. Mommy dearest never mentioned you."

"What?"

"Your twin brother, that whole sad thing? Some family's ski boat propeller meatgrindered through him? Yeah, guess who was skiing for their very first time that day, had a panic attack in all that sweet sweet blood, nearly drowned when he got some of your brother's intestines or thigh meat in his mouth?"

"Jamie?"

"For every prank there's an equal and much fucked-upper re-prank. I'm quoting you here. Think you got a C on that one, for language."

Izzy's world is collapsing a little bit. Her POV narrowing, her breathing deep, her blood loud in her ears, her mind

→ creating that black and white lake scene. The blood behind the boat. A young Jamie falling down into it. The bloody water going into his eyes, his nose, his mouth, staining him once and for all.

"That's right, killer," Lindsay says. "You created your own monster. Isn't that the way it always goes, though?"

Izzy climbs back into the world. *Makes* herself climb back.

"It was him—it was him at the party."

"No," Lindsay smiles, "*last* night he was with your little friend. Last night was—scroll down some, I think I forwarded it to him. He was supposed to delete it—*I* did—but he was sentimental, you know? Wanted souvenirs, all that."

Izzy scrolls down to a text from Lindsay. With an attachment. She hits play.

It's a video of that girl passed out by the toilet. Then of Billie Jean in the mirror, fitting the belt around his neck. Then sneaking around to Bogey and April on the bed, looking out the window at the party before angling the phone down onto his sword, waggling it like a giant penis.

"Jake," Izzy says.

"Everybody wants a little piece of the action," Lindsay says. "*This* action anyway. Which just begs the question. Do you? Maybe we took care of dear old Daddy together, right? Has there even been a double final girl?"

"*The Burning.*"

"That was boys, Izzy. Boys don't count. Everybody *expects* them to kill the baddie."

"We *did* take care of him together."

"Well. Maybe *I* say it, though. Then you get a starring role in this movie. The quirky little sidekick. How about it, yeah? We can be stars together. The homecoming queen and the—the . . . what is it you want to be?"

"Crystal's queen, now."

"*She's not shit!*"

"Anyway," Izzy says, dropping the phone, coming up with a

pitchfork, which she's apparently had all along, never mind what it was doing in a blind horse's stall. "I may hate my dad, but I never tried to kill him."

"You saw him," Lindsay says, not worried about the pitchfork. "He was trying to kill *me*."

"The first time, though? When you were the 'only one' to find him in his stall?"

"Oh," Lindsay says. "That. What could be worse than a girl's dream horse nearly killing her daddy, right? You've got to get the sympathy on your side before you get all violent. Then anything you do, it's justified."

"You stole him from the hospital."

"It's not shoplifting if he's family."

"People aren't objects," Izzy says, "they're not devices. People are people."

"And you and I should get along so *aw*-fully, right?" Lindsay says, smiling, really showing her crazy now. She looks down to the pitchfork Izzy's still holding like a bayonet, says, "Well? If we're going to do this let's—"

Izzy races forward with it.

Like Lindsay's not ready, though.

She loops the tines of the pitchfork with the cable, redirects it, pulling Izzy into her rising knee.

Izzy's head snaps back trailing blood, and, as easy as that, Lindsay loops the rest of the cable around her neck, hauls Izzy

→ over to the tall chute, all the ropes dizzying up into heaven.

She reaches up for a smallish hook, small enough for the cable, and ties it, wrenches Izzy up by the neck, strangling her, Izzy kicking, kicking, her boot finally lucking onto the big hook, putting some of her weight there. But it can't last.

"Hey," Lindsay says, stepping back, Izzy barely balanced, "this is all *Saw*, right? Here, the poetry part."

What she reaches back for is a machete. Which she angles over, lining it up on Izzy's leg, finally slicing it right through the meat above her right knee.

She steps back to appraise her work, nods.

"Billie Jean kills again," she says, simply. "Or maybe this is more

John Doe? Anyway, when you get tired of *almost* dying, just take *this*"—tapping the machete—"and cut *that*"—the big hook's thick rope. "It'll . . . well. You saw what happened to your little friend at the game? Something like that, yeah. But don't think of it like it's a decapitation. Think of it like immortality. You'll be a famous victim. Those little girls in junior high'll all be coloring their hair to be like you. Shopping in the boy's section, the military surplus store, Goodwill."

Izzy's still kicking, still digging at the cable in her neck, her leg bleeding fast, but still,

→ her swinging POV can look past Lindsay, to Wildfire, screaming.

And past that, down through the stalls, to Billie Jean unfolding from the rafters he pulled himself up into.

" . . . looks like Daddy learned a new trick," she just manages to get out, and

→ Lindsay turns around, holds her hands to her mouth to cover her shrieking laugh.

"Sorry," she says to Izzy, reaching forward for the machete, but Izzy spins painfully away,

→ leaving Lindsay to glom a hay hook off the post, run with it to Wildfire.

She unties the rope hitching him to a ring in the wall then backs off, slices down across his ass with her hook hand.

"Get him," she says, and Wildfire runs blind the same way the other horses did.

This time, though, Billie Jean's had enough.

He steps forward to meet Wildfire, bringing the sword all the way up from hell, and, like we were all secretly wanting that first time, he mostly decapitates the horse.

It keeps running past, its head just hanging on, its shoulder crashing into the door, shaking the whole barn.

"*Wildfire!*" Lindsay calls out, in pain, and is scrabbling away now, Billie Jean approaching steadily.

She turns, her back to the wall, Billie Jean jamming the sword into the wood right by her head.

Lindsay falls away, swings her hay hook at Billie Jean when he comes at her next.

He bats it away.

She falls against another wall, almost gets skewered, and finally lucks onto the ladder, pulls herself up it.

Billie Jean stands there a moment, watching her, then follows, leaving Izzy strangling out on her cable, her legs kicking free, her eyes wet and bloodshot, her

→ POV mostly on the ceiling.

The fight going on up there, hay dust sifting down through the cracks.

And then the fight goes higher.

Either that or she's dying.

But—but—

→ her hand, it's scrabbling down along her right leg.

She rips the machete free, lets her neck take the full weight of the cord while she slices up at it with the blade.

Finally she connects, but it's a cable, not a rope.

She strips the vinyl coating off, taking it down to metal, and is nearly dead now, her lips blue, her nose bleeding, eyes shot red, but then she swings wildly one more time, just manages to nick the rope right above the hook her cable's on.

The close-up of the rope twines out for long moments, finally snaps.

Izzy crashes to the floor gasping, coughing, not able to breathe.

And then a lit lantern crashes onto the floor beside her, its flames breathing out for anything it can find.

Izzy, still dry-heaving, looks up for what's next.

It's Billie Jean.

He's tumbling down fast, is going to hit her, she saved herself just to have him fall on, smash her into the—

But no.

That big hook, it catches under Billie Jean's head, stops him all at once with a jerk, so he's swaying back and forth, is that dummy from the pep-rally.

Izzy stands, still holding her throat, and looks up, her POV seeing nothing. Nothing.

"Boop," she says painfully, pinching out the idea of Lindsay up there.

She looks across to Billie Jean then, and of course his hand stabs out at her, has her by her throat.

Until the sword comes down into the top of his head, cuts through his spinal cord, the point coming out the seat of his pants, then dripping dark blood down into space.

Izzy guides his hand down, is breathing hard now, can see and hear spotlights and headlights and helicopters outside the barn, their hot light shining through in crazy, probing slats.

Izzy looks up the shaft again, takes a step and collapses over her right knee, cutting us

→ a minute or two ahead, to her rubbing the last velcro strap in place.

Of Billie Jean's leg brace.

She stands on it and it holds.

She looks up to him and calmly rips the sparkly B from her chest, pushes it into him.

It's not for "Brittney" anymore. It's for Billie Jean.

Next she collects the machete, uses it to pull down another of the big hooks, the

→ close-up of her boot stepping up onto it just like Ripley would have.

And then she reaches across, cuts a rope with one dramatic swipe, her hook pulling her up so that the last thing we see, it's Billie Jean's mask, slipping up off his head, Izzy taking it with her,

→ her POV now angling over through those eyeholes to study Lindsay, standing in the hay door at the very top of the barn.

Her dress is torn, she's bleeding, but every light out there, it's hot on her, it's drinking her in, her shadow huge across Izzy.

But Izzy's walking up out of it.

Her POV approaches steadily, her bloody hands coming up to Lindsay's shoulders, pulling her back to speak into her ear: "Virgins are the only ones who can do it right," she says, "and guess what I am," then pushes

→ the close-up of the machete out through Lindsay's sculptured chest, saying it over her shoulder: "Welcome to the Golden Age, bitch,"

→ Lindsay's rag doll of a body toppling out through the hay door, falling through the sky for hours, it seems like, finally slamming down not on a pipe or in a plow or on a hood, and not into the spinning blades of the helicopter parked there for some reason, but just onto the ground at Dante's feet, crunching into it headfirst and permanent, her body folding into itself like a slinky, so we can go

→ close on her face, on her eye, dilating out into the real death, which is always the last one you were expecting, and, looking back up, the barn is a firestorm now, a pyre, a bonfire, those sparks trailing up into the sky—

→ "Stratford," Dante says, half in thanks, half in farewell, and we're

→ back with those sparks, are floating around while we tune in crackly snatches of radio news:
"—last night at a house party four teens lost their lives in what can only be described as a massacre of Hollywood proportions, each death more grisly than the last, and coming right on the heels of the campground murders of two weekends ago—"
"—release of the name of the officer is pending notification of the family, though—"
"—word is just coming in about a grisly scene at a local residence, resulting in the death of not one but—"
"—the families of those six high school students have asked that remembrances and memoriums be left in their names at—"
"—local police are reticent to allow the possibility of a connection between that weekend and last night, but townspeople—"
"—and what kind of homecoming is that, right? Was that a halftime show or a horror movie? I mean, I was never royalty myself,

of course, but when I was—"

"—related news, long-time custodian Carl Wakefield, former student of Danforth High School in what locals refer to as its glory years, well as we all know he suffered massive—"

"—and the principal is apparently unavailable for comment—"

"—bodies are stacking up in Rivershead—"

"—supposedly a book deal—"

"—photos are already circulating—"

"—shook this local community to its agricultural roots—"

"—citzens have been quoted as saying that perhaps their town is cursed—"

"—people are going to remember the name 'Lindsay Baker'—"

"—it all started with Michael Jackson—"

"—something about a Halloween truck, that none of this would have happened if it hadn't—"

"Will the violence stop, though? Is it finally over?"

Beat, beat. Just drifting in those sparks, then:

"I mean, if every class tries to outdo the class before it, right? Then what the *hell* can we hope for next year? I ask you that," sending us falling back down through those dancing orange sparks,

→ hissing into the wet grass of the football field, the scoreboard still on but that's to the side.

Where we're looking is that announcer's booth at the top of the stands, so dark.

We ready ourselves for what the genre demands, for what we've paid for here, what we're expecting, but still, that bloody palm slapping hard up against the glass from the inside, paired with a scream from who knows where—from *Rivershead*—it straightens our backs, it quickens our breath, it stabs our hands out for somebody else's, so that, when we pan over to the scoreboard, we can smile—we made it through, *we're* the final girl—that Period indicator rolling ponderously over from *I* to *II*, then making it to *III* somehow, then gathering momentum, cycling higher and higher, too fast, a Roman numeral blur these lights were never designed for, delivering us right to

COLLEGE

A classroom, the big kind, that same one they always use.

Up-front on a huge screen is a paused frame of Jason at his most butchery, and in front of that is a youngish prof trying to disguise his good looks with the standard-issue tweed coat and specs. He's staring up at Jason, now turning to his captive class, his hands behind his back, his eyes glittering with forbidden knowledge.

Hugh Grant?

It doesn't matter.

We're in his POV, panning the class, just seeing the usual suspects and in-jokes and cameos—maybe even a dingy, striped sweater—and, slowly, starting at the boots so we can see her leg's healed, there's Izzy, a year or so older. We can tell by her hair, her new friends, how comfortable she is at the center of them. How much her life has evidently improved since we saw her last.

"And," the professor's asking now, dragging it out for pedagogic effect, "and, what is it that every killer these days must first and foremost have, before everything else?"

"*A remake!*" some guy calls down, like this is a pep-rally.

"Close, close," the professor says, nodding up to that student in thanks and strolling across the stage, peering out for the better answer.

"A sequel?" somebody else asks.

The professor shakes his head no, sadly. But close, close.

"Blood!" a guy in back yells, already laughing at himself.

"Goes without saying," the prof says back, not even bothering to look up to this guy. "Though we could all learn something from Tobe Hooper."

"Breasts!" a different-but-same joker calls out, to muffled laughs.

"Once upon a time, sure," the professor says, watching the toe of his left foot go back and forth, back and forth, but when the chuckles don't die he peers up under his romantic-comedy bangs. "These days it's about *titillation*, not . . . well."

The class loves this even more. And him.

"Prequel?" another student tries, biting her lip, hoping she's right.

"Getting hotter, getting hotter," the professor says, stopping to balance on the heels of his loafers again, but this time looking up to

→ Izzy, staring right back at him.

The professor nods to her, graciously giving her the floor.

"Izzy Stratford," he calls, as if announcing her. "We're lucky to have you here today."

"Lucky to be here," Izzy says, twirling a blue-tinted curl of hair.

The professor turns back around to appraise Jason up on the screen, and speaks loud now because he's facing away: "Tell us what every slasher needs, Izzy,"

→ and like that we shuffle at impossible speed through the key moment of every kill from that homecoming week a year ago, even including the sheriff, and end up back on all the flowers and pictures and beer bottles left in front of the chained-shut double doors of Danforth High School.

"An excellent backstory," Izzy voices over, and

→ we're back in the classroom with her, her hands churched over her mouth, that pin-drop kind of silence rippling back and forth, everybody looking down at the professor, still with his back to them.

"Well, Doc?" the joker calls out, the tension just ratcheting up higher, to a screech, almost.

In answer, and smoother than any criminal, the professor slides his left loafer back into the first part of a moonwalk, keeps it there long enough to pop his collar up.

The class erupts, papers in the air, #2 pencils spinning slow and deadly past faces, feet stomping, a bra drifting down from who knows where, "Billie Jean" rolling into a chant under all this, a lone lighter reaching up above, flicking on, and where we go is tight on Izzy's hands, falling away from her mouth. From her small, lip-biting grin.

"*Just you fucking wait,*" she says under all that sound, and we rush away from her, go jangly and backwards up the stairs faster than we know we can, push out into the hall, the door shutting back in front of us, the just-made sign swinging on the knob:

Slasher 101

→ but the top right corner's torn, is already letting go now that the door's being pushed open again, just wide enough for a hand to sneak its way through, hang a wicked Billie Jean mask on the knob.

Class is in session.

Now turn off the lights.

PIECES AND PARTS

A slightly older Ben is in the back of Dante's car, and there's red paint all over him. Dante's easing them down the road. To the station is the idea. Meaning Ben really is trying to leave his mark.

"Remember homecoming that time?" Ben says up to Dante.

"What about it?" Dante says into the rearview.

Ben shrugs, looks out his side glass.

"When Crystal Blake, you know," Ben says. "When she showed her goods like that. You were the only one to keep your head."

"So?"

"So how'd you do it, man?"

Dante smiles wide, and we're right on his face for him to say it: "Who says I'm into girls?"

Dante's at a convenience store deep in the dark hours, taking a report from a flustered clerk, his POV studying the men's room door. Like it's calling his name.

"So he didn't even want the money, you say?" Dante's saying, already bored with this.

"No, man, that's just it," the clerk's saying in wonder. "It was like, I don't know. All he wanted was those burritos, like."

Ben and his friends at the creek by the bridge, the day they brought the black sword there and ground it sharp. They're all so young, still.

Ben's looking up and up into that shadow falling across them, and it's a mummy in a letterman's jacket, just standing there in the dying light, waiting.

"I'm never coming back here," Ben says.

The front of Izzy's old house, her mom and dad out front, trying to Iwo Jima the new piece of metalwork up.

Finally it tilts over, finds its gravity.

From the side, it's nothing, just twisted metal, but coming around the front, it's . . . Michael Jackson up on his toes, one hand pulling his fedora down over his eyes.

Behind him, Izzy's dad takes his wife's hand in his.

A POV floating down along the cliff, to the river, and then up it some, where we haven't been.

To that Halloween truck, half under water.

Something thunks down there and a horse head mask floats free, its big eye just staring, but we don't go with it on its journey.

We're still with the truck.

Waiting for a rotted hand to hook itself over the top of the cargo box.

What surfaces instead is that turtle.

It climbs onto the top corner of the box, into the sun, and cranes its wet black eyes up, up, so we look too, don't know what to make of the deep splash that follows.

Just that it won't be the last.

THE LAST FINAL GIRL

ACKNOWLEDGMENTS

This all starts in junior high in Wimberley, Texas. Every Friday night a bunch of us would plunder the horror shelves at the video store then pile into David O'Connor's garage, watch Michael and Jason and Freddy until David's dad would sneak outside, put on a mask or some knife-fingers and bang on the garage door at the perfect time to send us out running through the trees, screaming through the darkness, smiling through the tears. It's what the slasher's all about. And thanks to Ryan van Cleave, for pulling me to a certain dollar theater in 1996, in Tallahasee, Florida. I was there for six nights after, paying my dollar, waiting for Billy to say it again. And thanks to Joe Ferrer and Danny Broyles and Rob Weiner and Jesse Lawrence and Adam Cesare and Mike Hance and Rob Bass and Jesse Bullington and Jeremy Robert Johnson, for all the discussions, all the help, all the redirects. All the horror. Thanks to Cameron Pierce, for believing in this book, and to Matthew Revert, for the best cover yet, and to Kate Garrick, my agent, for making it all happen. And, as always, to my wife, Nancy, for sleeping on the couch beside me once upon a time in 1999 in a two-hundred dollar a month house, so I could keep watching horror movie after horror movie, not be scared because I knew you were right there with me.

ABOUT THE AUTHOR

Stephen Graham Jones is the author of *Zombie Bake-Off*, *Demon Theory*, *The Ones that Got Away*, *It Came from Del Rio*, *Growing Up Dead in Texas*, and probably twice that many more. Stephen's been an NEA Fellow, a Stoker Award finalist, and has won the Texas Institute of Letters award for fiction. He lives in Boulder, Colorado, and teaches in the MFA programs at CU Boulder and UCR Palm Desert.

ALSO FROM LAZY FASCIST PRESS

A PRETTY MOUTH
BY MOLLY TANZER

"The Calipash line, as I am sure all the other members of this club well know, is ... tainted. Members of that family tend to be eccentric if not totally insane, and from their origins to the present day there have been reports of Calipashes engaging in such behaviors as voluntary demonic possession, murder, necromancy in the classical and modern sense of the word, black magics of all kinds, sexual perversion, cannibalism, and, perhaps counterintuitively, militant vegetarianism."

"This is form and content and diction and tone and imagination all looking up at the exact same moment: when Molly Tanzer claps once at the front of the classroom."

—STEPHEN GRAHAM JONES

"A Pretty Mouth is a fine and stylish collection that pays homage to the tradition of the weird while blazing its own sinister mark. Tanzer's debut is as sharp and polished as any I've seen."

—LAIRD BARRON, author of *The Croning*

"If Hieronymus Bosch and William Hogarth had together designed a Fabergé egg, the final result could not be more beautifully and deliciously perverse than what awaits the readers in A Pretty Mouth. Molly Tanzer's first novel is a witty history of the centuries-long exploits of one joyfully corrupt (and somewhat moist) Calipash dynasty, a family both cursed and elevated by darkness of the most squamous sort. This is a sly and sparkling jewel of a book, and I can't recommend it enough—get A Pretty Mouth in your hands or tentacles, post-haste, and prepare to be shocked, charmed, and (somewhat moistly) entertained!"

—LIVIA LLEWELLYN, author of *Engines of Desire*

"Had the nineteenth century really been like this—with the flounces and corsets and blood and tentacles and whatnot—we'd all be dead by now. Unlucky us, but lucky you, Dear Reader, as you are alive to read this book."

—NICK MAMATAS, author of *Bullettime*

"A Pretty Mouth is many things; erudite, hilarious, profane, moving, learned, engaging, horrific, terrifying, and profound. Molly moves through the multi-forms of prose like a shark in wine-dark seas, rife with allusion, deep in emotion, and sometimes giving you a little salty-mouth. A fantastic collection and not one to be missed."

—JOHN HORNOR JACOBS, author of *This Dark Earth*

AVAILABLE AT AMAZON.COM

LAZY FASCIST 2012

2013

Zombie Sharks with Metal Teeth by Stephen Graham Jones
The Collected Works of Noah Cicero Vol. I by Noah Cicero
Rontel by Sam Pink
Basal Ganglia by Matthew Revert
The Humble Assessment by Kris Saknussemm
Colony Collapse by J.A. Tyler
Asshole by Patrick Wensink

Plus many more!

CPSIA information can be obtained
at www.ICGtesting.com
Printed in the USA
LVHW030108270821
696159LV00011B/878

9 781621 050513